STAGES OF LIFE

STAGES OF LIFE

A Triumphant Story of an African Child

UCHE N. KALU

STAGES OF LIFE
A TRIUMPHANT STORY OF AN AFRICAN CHILD

This is a work of fiction. All of the characters, names, incidents, organizations, and dialogue in this novel are either the products of the author's imagination or are used fictitiously.

iUniverse books may be ordered through booksellers or by contacting:

iUniverse
1663 Liberty Drive
Bloomington, IN 47403
www.iuniverse.com
1-800-Authors (1-800-288-4677)

Because of the dynamic nature of the Internet, any web addresses or links contained in this book may have changed since publication and may no longer be valid. The views expressed in this work are solely those of the author and do not necessarily reflect the views of the publisher, and the publisher hereby disclaims any responsibility for them.

Any people depicted in stock imagery provided by Thinkstock are models, and such images are being used for illustrative purposes only.
Certain stock imagery © Thinkstock.

ISBN: 978-1-5320-3354-4 (sc)
ISBN: 978-1-5320-3355-1 (e)

Library of Congress Control Number: 2017915095

Print information available on the last page.

iUniverse rev. date: 12/13/2017

The book is dedicated to my wife, Mercy, and my children, Daniel, Michael, Rebecca, and Benjamin.

Acknowledgments

I would like to thank those who contributed in one way or another to help me produce this book. I also thank God for giving me the wisdom and the inspiration to write the book.

Chapter 1

THE BIRTH OF CHIDI

The hamlet was so quiet and lonely. Except a few children who played around the compound. Anyone who visited the village might have thought the inhabitants had been taken captive.

It was the beginning of the farming season. Everybody had gone to clear the farmland to prepare for the new planting season, except Uloma who was alone in the house. She was filled with anxiety because she was expecting to deliver her child very soon. Her husband had gone to clear his farmland. He'd promised his wife that he would return soon, but the nature of his work wouldn't permit him to return as soon as he had promised.

Suddenly, Uloma felt the baby moving in her belly. She groaned in agony as the baby continued to move vigorously. No one was there to help her as she struggled. Finally, she gave birth and collapsed on the floor.

A woman who was passing by Uloma's compound heard the cry of a baby. As she walked closer to the house, she asked in a loud voice, "Is anybody there?" Her voice echoed throughout the compound. "Is anybody there?" she repeated.

There was no response. Quickly, she entered the house and found both Uloma and her child in a terrible situation. Uloma lay in a pool of blood on the floor next to her baby. Her face was covered with perspiration, and her entire body shook as if she were suffering from an acute fever. Quickly, the woman took the baby, removed the cord still attached to the mother, and cleaned the baby. When she turned around, Uloma was still lying on the floor, but she was dead.

The stranger was confused and afraid; she didn't know what to do. At that moment, Uloma's husband, Udo, returned home. He was completely deranged, and he wept bitterly. People heard him crying hopelessly and came to see what was wrong. Soon they all understood that Udo's wife had died during childbirth.

A few days later, Udo buried his wife. He decided to allow the baby to be taken to the village nursery, where he could receive proper care as an infant. The nursery had been in existence for more than ten years. The Umueze community built the nursery to provide care for babies abandoned by careless mothers who had fallen victim to unwanted pregnancies. Members of the community compensated people who took care of the babies.

Three months after Uloma was buried, the Umueze community set aside a day to commemorate her life. On that day, the elders, chiefs, and people of the village all came together. The observance ceremony was held in Udo's compound. The Eze One, or the first king of the village, was at the head of the gathering. According to the belief of the villagers, food had to be prepared for the dead. When the people ate those foods prepared for the event, many believed that the dead were eating as well. According to their beliefs, in a situation where the ritual fails to be observed, the spirit of the dead person will rise to haunt the living ones.

Uloma's funeral wasn't observed like a man's funeral since the villagers believed men to be superior to women. Hence, in this respect, women's funerals were usually observed in a low profile. Therefore, only a few activities were observed for Uloma.

Since Uloma's death, it seemed Udo lived the life of a bachelor who hadn't yet dreamed of getting married. At home he prepared his food and did domestic work a woman usually did. He visited his son at the nursery each week after working on his farm.

One day he planned to visit his son and packed some food and gifts for him. As he was leaving the compound, he heard Uloma's voice, but he was mistaken. It was all in his mind. He never ceased to think about her. Sometimes almost every figure in sight appeared to be his wife. Even on the fourth night after her death, Udo dreamed Uloma was crying because she hadn't eaten any food on the day she died. That was one of the reasons that led them to observe the burial ceremony because the people believed that when food is served and people eat at the burial, Uloma's spirit would be satisfied.

As these thoughts passed through his mind, Udo thought he heard his wife's voice again. This time he turned around to see who was mimicking her. To his surprise, it was Alice, the woman who had helped to save his son on the day he was born. Alice had never stopped caring for Udo's son; she had just visited his son at the nursery and wanted to talk to Udo about the child's well-being. As Alice came closer to the compound, she saw Udo and smiled.

He remembered her kindness to his family on the day his wife died. He knew Alice cared for his family and was thinking about how he could show his appreciation for the kindness she'd shown.

Alice was a widow who had lost her husband to a heart attack nearly two years before. Since her husband had passed away, she had been living alone and had recently decided to remarry. She hoped God would provide her with another man who would be like her late husband. She was able to make a living from the money and property her husband had left her after his death.

At the moment Alice walked closer to Udo, she imagined him as somebody who would care for her. They simply greeted each other and talked about his son, Chidi. Afterward, Udo decided to visit Chidi at the nursery. Chidi was growing to look like him. Udo became sad when he looked at him because Chidi reminded him of Uloma, so he grieved for her in his mind. "If death could be defeated by physical strength, I would have defeated it to save my wife's life," he said to himself.

His son's loss of his mother reminded him of his father, Uke, who had died and left him and his mother behind. After his father died, they'd suffered tremendously to make ends meet. To provide for the family, his mother took on various odd jobs. On one occasion, he and his mother went to clear farmland for a man in their village. The man hired his mother to work for only a few pennies a day. They worked tirelessly to finish the job assigned to her. That was how his mother made money to provide food for the family. Udo remembered that it was this type of hardship that had taught him a great lesson about life, so he prayed that such misfortune wouldn't fall on his son. Though Uloma was dead, he couldn't allow Chidi to suffer if he could help it.

Udo always wanted to give his son what he hadn't

received from his father, such as an education. But if he couldn't afford to send Chidi to school, he would teach him how to create a better life for himself in the future.

Almost three years passed since Chidi began living in the nursery. Udo still lived alone in his house. One day, Udo and his friend Mazi Ugo went to visit Chidi and to bring him back home. It would be a happy moment for Mazi Udo when Chidi returned home to live with him.

Mazi Ugo was Udo's only close friend. He was the only one in whom Udo confided. Whenever he needed to discuss anything important, he consulted Mazi Ugo for advice. That's why he invited Mazi Ugo to accompany him when he went to bring Chidi back home from the nursery.

A ceremony was usually held whenever a child was mature enough to be retrieved from the nursery back to his or her parents' home. Udo invited Mazi Ugo to go with him to celebrate Chidi's departure back to his father's house.

They brought food, kola nuts, and palm wine to celebrate the occasion. Udo had informed the people at the nursery in advance that they would be coming that day to retrieve his son. So they were all waiting for him and Mazi Ugo to arrive. They arrived later on.

During the ceremony, Mazi Ugo brought out the kola nuts and opened the ceremony. In his presentation, he made these statements: "We are inviting our ancestors to join us in this gathering. Whosoever brings forth kola nut has brought life. Those who joined in sharing the kola will also enjoy life. We beseech our ancestors to bring prosperity to the giver and those who will follow in the breaking of the kola nut. The child whom we have come to take back to his father's house ... protect his life and the life of everyone who is here."

Everyone responded by saying, "Ise-e-e-e," which means "so it shall be." After the incantation, Mazi Ugo gave a kola nut to a young man, James, who had come to the ceremony. James was about twenty years old and one of the residents of the nursery. Actually, he was one of the first babies raised at the nursery. After he grew up, no one had come to claim him, so he had to live at the nursery and assist the nurses with the younger children. At the end of the ceremony, Mazi Ugo gave the nurses some money and gifts to show his appreciation for their help with Chidi. Afterward, Udo and Chidi went home.

Chapter 2

COPING WITH A NEW HOME

Chidi didn't find it difficult to adapt to his new environment. He made friends in the village and played with them frequently. However, he cried for his mother whenever any of his playmates started fighting him. His constant cry became a problem to his father because it reminded him of his late wife. He always tried to stop Chidi from playing with other children if the play caused him to cry, but it never worked; the situation simply became worse.

After some time, Udo decided he should get married again so he would have someone to help him with Chidi. Actually, he considered Alice, the woman who had saved Chidi at birth, but Udo had a difficult time getting in touch with her.

One day the women of the village were celebrating women's day. It was the day when the women of Umueze came together to discuss the issues facing the village and to talk about their family problems.

On this special day, women came from all the neighboring villages. Several men also came to celebrate, including Udo. While he stood at the opposite side of the house, he noticed Alice was among the women seated across the way. He called her to come over and talk with him. She went to him, and they greeted each other cordially.

Udo looked at her as he began to talk to her. "I came here, hoping to see you and to talk to you. I thought you would be at the house the day Chidi came back home."

She smiled at him gracefully as she responded. "You told me about his return, but I couldn't come that day. I was busy at home. How is he doing at home?"

"He is fine," Udo answered in a low voice. "But he has been worrying me."

"Worrying you?" Alice said in surprise. She had thought Udo would be happy with Chidi after he was nursed back to life.

"You see, Chidi always cries for his mother anytime the other children tease him. I expect him to cry for his father, who is always with him, since his mother is no more around!" Udo said as he held his head down.

Alice smiled at Udo as she responded to his remark. "A child usually cries for his mother, not for his father. That is a fact. Children always do that. There is nothing wrong with that, and you shouldn't worry about it." Then, as she began thinking about

Chidi, she said, "Poor Chidi. It is unfortunate for a little child like him to start experiencing a motherless life. I shall take some time to visit him."

"Please do so," Udo said happily. "I am tired of this problem. When do you think you will visit him?"

Alice thought for a moment. "Ah, I think I will visit him on Friday after work."

"That would be wonderful. Then I'll see you on Friday," he replied with a smile as he stared at her. Afterward, they went back to their seats.

It seemed that Udo's plan would work out. He believed Alice would agree to marriage if he proposed to her. He knew she had developed the same feelings for him. Almost everyone had notice how Alice cared for him, but it was difficult for her to tell him how she really felt. African women don't believe it's right for a woman to approach a man first, even if she feels deeply in love. Some women feel that in doing so, men would take them for granted and not to take their love seriously. In Alice's case, she believed the love would be strong when a man expressed his feelings to the woman first.

In the meantime, Udo started dreaming about how things would change in his life once he married Alice. In particular, he thought about how she could help Chidi grow.

As Friday approached, Udo decided not to go to his farm since Alice had promised to visit him and

Chidi. He was at home, cleaning his compound. While in his room, he heard a knock at the door. It must be Alice, he thought, but it was his friend Mazi Ugo instead. He had come to visit Udo and his son. Mazi Ugo hadn't visited them since the day Udo brought Chidi home from the nursery. When he opened the door, the two friends greeted each other warmly.

"Welcome, Mazi Ugo," Udo said.

"How are you and your child?" Mazi Ugo asked.

"We are doing well," Udo answered. He offered his friend a seat and sat down next to him. Afterward, he asked Chidi to come and greet Mazi Ugo.

Chidi walked into the house from outside, where he had been playing with other children. "Oh, Chidi, you are so dirty. You must have been playing in the sand with your friends again. Go and greet Mazi Ugo," Udo said diligently.

After he had greeted Mazi Ugo, Chidi ran back outside to join his friends again to play. Mazi Ugo turned to Udo and said, "This child is approaching school age. Why not put him in school?"

"That is what I am planning to do when the village school reopens for the next session," Udo explained.

"He looks very healthy, and I hope that he is going to be brilliant in school," Mazi Ugo added.

Udo wanted to say something, but he paused for

a second; he just remembered that he hadn't offered his friend anything. Quickly, he asked, "What can I offer you?"

"Anything that will be good for my body."

Mazi Ugo chuckled.

Suddenly, Udo went into his room and returned with bitter kola nuts and alligator pepper with some drinks. Whenever kola nuts are presented, the ancestors are the first to be invited to share in the breaking and eating of the nuts. According to tradition, Mazi Ugo took the kola nuts and made some incantation, calling on the ancestors to join in the breaking and sharing of the kola nuts. Then he broke them into small pieces.

While they shared the kola nuts, the two men discussed many issues. During their discussion, Mazi Ugo asked Udo why he hadn't remarried since his wife died. He advised him to marry someone who would take care of him and his son.

"I have a plan for that, and I will let you know when it materializes," Udo said. They continued discussing other things, and after some time, Mazi Ugo departed and went home.

Soon after Mazi Ugo left, there was a second knock at the door. When Udo opened the door, Alice stood there, smiling at him. "Where is my son, Chidi?" she asked. She remembered when the nurses at the Nursery had called her Chidi's mother because she often visited him. They'd thought she was his real mother.

Next, Udo said, "Chidi is outside, playing with other children."

"Oh, is he still spending a lot of time playing with his friends?" she asked.

"Should I prevent him from playing with his friends? I cannot prevent him from playing," Udo exclaimed. Afterward, he went outside to get Chidi. When they entered the house, Udo told him to greet their visitor.

Chidi walked to Alice and greeted her. As she was talking to him, Udo went behind the house to harvest some fruit. Later, he returned to the house with some oranges and offered them to Alice. "This is for your refreshment; I hope you'll like them," Udo said.

"Thank you," Alice responded. As she was peeling the oranges, Udo told his son to go and join his friends to play outside. That was when Udo began to tell Alice how he felt about her.

Alice didn't say much about what he told her; rather, she wanted him to give her some time to think about it. She thought that if he really meant some of the things he had said to her, he must be really interested in marrying her. Consequently, she didn't want to yield easily to his request. She wanted to take time to build their relationship so that whenever they were married, Udo would value her love and not take her for granted. She'd been married once before and didn't have a child. At this time, her priority was to have children.

Chapter 3

THE MARRIAGE PROPOSAL

Mazi Obieke was having dinner in his house with his two wives and children when Alice came to visit him. He was Alice's uncle, a younger brother to her late father. It was he who'd assumed his brother's role in the family after his brother died. Therefore, Alice always consulted him for advice. She wanted to know whether he would support her decision to marry Udo.

"Please have a seat, my daughter," he said. "I haven't seen you for a while. Is everything all right with you?"

"Yes, everything is fine," she explained.

Mazi Obieke smiled as he continued, "I saw you the other day when the women of Umueze were having a meeting. You were so busy enjoying yourself with your friends."

"Why didn't you say something when you saw me?" she asked.

"I knew you were busy, and it would have been unfair to disturb you as you were holding conversation with your group." He expressed his feelings with deep respect. Mazi Obieke was very protective of his own. During his youth, he had been a womanizer and always thought that every man who came around was coming after his sisters. He watched other men like a hawk watching its baby birds. Whenever any man came around his sister, he chased the person away, because he didn't want anyone to mess with his sisters. He had three sisters and one brother.

He invited Alice to join the family dinner. After they had finished eating, the wives and children left the table so he could have a private time to talk with his niece.

Alice told him why she had come to visit him. He later assured her that Udo was a good man who had a great reputation in their village. "He is loving man who doesn't like trouble, an upright man as well," Mazi Obieke advised as he looked at Alice. He encouraged her to marry him if she was really in love with him, so Alice agreed to marry Udo after she had sought the support of her uncle.

Later, Mazi Obieke sent for Udo. When the messenger came to his house, Udo wasn't at home. He had gone to register his son at the village school. Fortunately for him, Udo met the messenger on his way back home.

On the previous day, Udo had gone to the school alone to inquire about his son's school registration and had been told to bring his son with him so the school could decide whether he had reached school age. He went back to the school the following day with Chidi.

When Udo got the message, he went to Mazi Obieke to discuss everything about the marriage. They agreed on the day he would come back to pay the bride-price. After meeting Mazi Obieke, Udo went to inform his friend, Mazi Ugo, about the marriage and to ask him to accompany him to meet with his in-laws on the day he would go to pay the bride-price.

Mazi Ugo was busy in his workshop when Udo came to see him. "I went to your house to look for you," Udo said, "but it was your daughter who told me to look for you at your workshop."

Mazi Ugo was a genius in carpentry. He made all sorts of woodcrafts—tables, stools, benches, coffins, and so many other things. His skills had made him famous in the village of Umueze. Some people had nicknamed him "The Woodpecker"; he was always working with wood.

Mazi Ugo took his friend back to his house. Both friends met and discussed all the matters concerning the bride-price and the marriage. Earlier, Udo had told his friend about the woman he was going to marry. Mazi Ugo was excited and asked, "Who is the lucky woman?"

"Her name is Alice; she is the daughter of Okafor, the elder brother of Mazi Obieke," he said.

"Oh, you mean the woman who lost her husband two years ago. Why did you choose to marry a secondhand woman?" Mazi Ugo asked.

"I have a reason for that," Udo continued. "There is a secret behind this marriage. I will disclose it to you. The woman has helped me so much in my life. She is the one I met in my house while she was trying to save Uloma and our son, Chidi. After Uloma died, she didn't give up; she took Chidi to the Nursery and devoted all her time and material to ensure the baby was nursed to life. The love she has for my family has convinced me to marry her," Udo explained solemnly.

When Mazi Ugo heard this, he changed his mind and supported the marriage.

"I have met her uncle, and he agreed to the bride-price and the marriage," Udo said. After he explained everything to his friend, Udo left and went home.

It was customary for the people of Umueze to hold the marriage festival at night. On the appointed evening of the marriage, Udo and his friend and other guests went to meet Udo's in-laws.

According to tradition, Mazi Ugo carried a pot of palm wine as they came to Mazi Obieke's house. All the in-laws had already gathered at Mazi Obieke's house, waiting for Mazi Ugo and his people to arrive. After they did, Mazi Ugo stood up to speak to the people. He brought the palm wine and the money for the bride-price; he handed them to the in-laws.

According to the custom and traditions of the land, the normal bride-price was seven shillings.

Mazi Obieke, who stood as a father to the bride, took the money and palm wine. The money was counted in front of everyone, and the transaction was complete. Then Mazi Obieke took the palm wine since he was the head of the in-laws. Next, he poured some of the wine in a calabash cup, drank a little, and then passed it to Alice to give to the man who was to be her husband.

Alice wasn't shy about the event. This wasn't her first time for such a ceremony. When she and her late husband had come to perform the same ceremony, she had been a young girl; thus, she'd felt shy to perform the ceremony. However, this time she went to Udo boldly and gave him a cup of wine. Immediately, as she gave the cup to Udo, everyone applauded to express their happiness and support.

There was a lot of entertainment before Udo and his friends went back home to receive the wife. After they had returned to the house, the people danced along with the new bride to take her to her husband. That was how Udo and Alice were married.

Alice started to experience life as a married woman for the second time. She expected better days in her new life. She dreamed of having her own children one day. She loved and treated Udo's son, Chidi, as her own. Not everyone knew he wasn't her son; only those told otherwise knew the difference.

Now Chidi was five years old and doing very well in school. He was in the first grade, and he always scored the highest on his examinations. Such performance made his teacher, Stanley Eze to admire him, so Mr. Eze advised Chidi's parents to encourage Chidi to continue his efforts in school.

Alice began sewing clothes so she could sell them to people in the village. Sometimes people brought material for her to sew for them. Her husband was still a farmer. He produced yams and other foodstuff in large quantities. He was well known throughout the village. Now that he had married Alice, they worked together to make a better life for their family. Each year Udo made a great harvest. His barn was filled with large yams, which he sold to people and other farmers. Alice also made some profit from her trade.

A year passed by, and she hadn't yet conceived a child. That fact made her worry very often. "It would be unnatural if a woman like me would spend the rest of her life without a child. I am getting old as the years go by. I'm afraid that I may not be able to have a baby as I grow older. I don't want to leave this life without a child," she murmured to herself.

Udo didn't know how much Alice needed a child because she never discussed the matter with him. Eventually, Udo noticed Alice was going through some problems when she refused to eat. When Udo realized what was amiss, he began to encourage her about the problem. He told her someday she would have a baby, but his advice didn't stop her worries. Alice's problem reminded Chief Udo of his own personal problem. "As people faces differ, so are their problems," Udo noted. Nobody would know anyone's problem until he or she was told.

Chief Udo hadn't told Alice about his two brothers who died before they were married. The older brother died at war, while the youngest one died from a mysterious illness at his young age. Chief Udo was the only surviving son of Uke. Chief Udo had decided to put the death of his brothers behind him. Another friend of Chief Udo, Chiko, had once invited him to a wake keeping for his sister who had died. He was there to support him. He used his loss as an experience to encourage others to move on with their lives. Udo advised Chiko to put the death of his sister behind him as Udo had done for his own lost brothers. The death of Chiko's sister was a great lost for Chiko, just as Udo's loss of his two brothers had been a great loss for Udo. He could relate the death of Chiko's sister to the loss of his own brothers.

"People who lost their loved ones know how hard it can be, unlike those who hadn't experienced the death of a loved one," Chief Udo would say. When stories of the dead ones were told, those not affected didn't take them seriously. It was always said that when somebody else's dead body was being hauled away, others would see it as if it were a log of wood being carried away because the deceased didn't relate to the person.

Chief Udo remembered when his brothers died; some came to support him, while others did not. The loss didn't mean much to them because they weren't related to his deceased brothers, and they had no reason to sympathize with him. As it's said. "What a mighty fallen," Udo remembered that day when the news came to them that his senior brother had been killed in the war. It was a sad moment in his family, since it was always said that the fall of a mighty tree was a reminder to those still standing that one day it would be their turn to fall. Those who may not care about another person's death would eventually experience their own death or that of their loved ones someday.

After Udo realized what his wife was going through for not conceiving a child at this time of her marriage, he was always there to support her.

Chapter 4

TROUBLE AT SCHOOL

Alice was preparing lunch in the kitchen when Chidi returned from school.

"Mother!" he said, beckoning her.

"My son, have you come back from school already? What is the matter?" She noticed Chidi wasn't happy about something, which was unlike him.

As Chidi walked closer, he replied slowly, "One of my schoolmates teased me, and she said to me that I was motherless. Is this true?"

Alice was surprised to hear that, and she questioned the veracity of the complaint. She put her arms around him to make him feel better. "That must be a joke, my son," she said. "I am your mother. Don't mind what they said to you in school. Go and change your clothes and get ready for lunch."

Chidi took his schoolbag into his bedroom.

Alice began to worry about Chidi. She believed it was too early at his age for the boy to know about the death of his mother; it might affect his behavior. After a few minutes, Chidi came to the table to eat his lunch. Whenever he ate his food, Alice stayed by his side to make him feel the closeness of a mother. The only time Chidi ate by himself was when Alice was in the kitchen, preparing dinner.

Later, Udo returned from the farm. Once Alice saw him walking toward the door, she left Chidi and went to the door to welcome him. They both greeted each other. She took his bag and went into the room. Udo walked to the table to see his son for a few minutes.

Chidi greeted him, and they began to talk. While he was chatting with his father, Chidi asked him the same question he had asked Alice, but Udo didn't understand what he meant. He responded by telling him children always say silly things to one another. Chidi took his father's advice and went to his room to study.

By this time, Alice had gone to the kitchen to prepare something for her husband. While Alice was in the kitchen, getting food ready, Udo was in the sitting room, thinking about what his son had just told him. After she came to the room, Udo told her what Chidi had said. She acknowledged that Chidi has told her as well. They talked about the matter for a moment, and Udo decided that he would take the complaint to the school and speak to the headmaster. He wanted such silly talk to stop.

The next day, he went to the village school. As he walked into the headmaster's office, the headmaster, Mr. Stephen, recognized him and greeted him. "Welcome to our school, Mr. Udo. What can I do for you?"

Udo cleared his throat. "I came to tell you about something that happened to my son yesterday in school."

"What happened?" the headmaster asked.

Udo said slowly, "One of your pupils teased Chidi and told him he was motherless. Although it may sound childish, the statement may have adverse effects on my son's behavior, and that's why I came to report the matter to you."

The headmaster was puzzled to hear such a comment. He apologized to Udo and promised to put a stop to such behavior.

The next day during the school morning assembly, the headmaster went to find out the student who had caused the trouble. Her name was Isabela. It was during this assembly that the headmaster invited Chidi to see him in his office after the assembly.

Chidi became nervous, because everyone knew Mr. Stephen as a severe disciplinarian. He didn't give any of his pupils a second chance when they misbehaved. Everyone at the school was aware of that fact, even the teachers. The pupils were always afraid of going to his office because they barely escaped being punished when called there for misbehavior. After thinking about the headmaster, Chidi became more frightened as he wondered what was about to happen.

Perhaps my teacher submitted my name to him as the best pupil in class, he thought. He became more worried as his classmates began to scare him. When the assembly was over, he went to see the headmaster. As he walked close to his office, he began to panic. He knocked on the office door and waited for a few minutes.

"Come in!" the headmaster yelled from inside. Chidi opened the door and reluctantly went in. The headmaster was sitting back in his chair and writing something when Chidi came in.

"Good morning, sir," Chidi said.

Mr. Stephen didn't respond immediately when Chidi came into his office, he was busy writing some notes. Chidi became nervous and started trembling.

Then the headmaster looked up and called his name. "Chidi! Did you tell your father that somebody in this school teased you?"

"No, sir. I didn't. It was my mother I told about it," he said in a frightened voice. Mr. Stephen wasn't pleased. He didn't want any problem in school to turn into a domestic problem before it could be resolved. He believed Chidi should have reported the matter to him first instead of taking the matter to his parents. The headmaster wasn't cheerful about the report. He turned to Chidi in a serious note and asked, "Who was the person who teased you?"

"It was one little girl in my class," Chidi replied.

"I mean her name. Don't you know her name?" Charlse Stephen asked.

Chidi didn't want to cause trouble, so he simply told him he couldn't remember her name. Mr. Stephen told him he would find the student by himself. After a short period, Chidi left his office.

After he returned to the classroom, his classmates asked him why Mr. Stephen had called him to his office; but he refused to talk to them about what had happened. Later, the headmaster discussed the matter with Chidi's teacher. The teacher later found the student who had teased Chidi. She was taken to the school garden to weed the grass as a punishment. That would teach other students not to tease anyone in their class anymore.

Chapter 5

THE GREAT CORONATION

Udo and his friend Mazi Ugo were to be made chiefs in their village. Their people wanted to honor them for their invaluable contributions to the development of Umueze.

Udo was a very hard-working farmer. He had won the title "King of Yams," which was given to the best yam producer in Umueze. He had also acquired many other titles in their village, such as the "Masquerade King." These titles made him popular in Umueze.

Mazi Ugo was also a good farmer, but he wasn't as great as his friend Udo. He was known mostly for his carpentry work.

On the day of the coronation, the village was filled with people from other villages. They all came to celebrate the occasion. Both friends were in their chieftaincy attire. They were marched from the village square to the king's palace, where the event was to take place.

People were dressed in their white vests, which had inscriptions on both sides. They said, "Eze One of Umueze," which means "The first chief of the village." That was the title given to Udo. His friend Mazi Ugo was called "Oka Ome of Umueze," which means "The trustworthy chief."

The two chiefs stood before the king, the supreme king of Umueze. He was sitting on his throne, dressed in his most outstanding attire. On this day, he was expected to be his most regal. As the new chiefs rose, the king walked to them, and they knelt in submission. A man approached the king with two crowns. The king collected both crowns from him and placed them on the heads of Udo and Mazi Ugo, one after the other. At this point, they were both declared chiefs in Umueze.

After the declarations, the crowd cheered and exalted the two new chiefs. To celebrate the coronation, they began to shoot the village gunpowder. After Udo and Ugo received the crowns, they raised their hands to the crowd in acceptance of their new titles. Immediately, people returned to the village square, where the reception was to take place. The people had prepared a lot of food, and all of them enjoyed themselves as they never had before.

The gunpowder continued to blast with heavy sounds as the events were in full swing. As part of the festivities, the village hunters emerged to demonstrate their shooting skills. Their target was to shoot the top of the mighty tree standing in the center of the village square. The leaves and tree branches started falling when the hunters shot the tree. In most cases, the hunters shot down birds such as vultures that perched on the treetops. When a vulture was shot down from a tree, the people believed the shooter would shoot bush meat the next time he went to hunt. Or so they believed.

The sounds of the guns were very intense at the time of the shooting demonstration. The children were afraid of the heavy sounds. They didn't come close until the shooting was all over; then they ran out to pick up the empty bullet shells.

The village also observed other traditional events, such as the masquerades, the women's dance, and many other events taking place that day. Everyone enjoyed the event. It was a lively occasion. Among the masquerades, there was an outstanding one called the "long masquerade." The name was given to it based on its appearance. At once, the masquerade would start to grow tall, and immediately it would start to shrink and adjust its height until it became completely short; nobody could recognize it anymore.

The Ekpe cult, a mystic society, owned the long masquerade. Only the male sons of Umueze who had reached the age of twenty were allowed to become members. It was mandatory for every male child of

Umueze to initiate into the Ekpe cult, a traditional group created for the young male of Umeze village to carter for themselves. Any male child of Umueze who failed to initiate into the cult wasn't allowed to participate in the village activities. Neither would he be allowed to participate in the village traditional marriage. Only members were allowed to receive an honor from the long masquerade during the year celebration or when one of their members died. The two newly installed chiefs were the members of the Ekpe cult. Chief Udo had the intention of initiating his own son when he reached the age of twenty.

The long masquerade was different from the other cults. It was observed as not only a cultural event but also a ceremonial event. It was usually observed when the village marked their seasonal events, such as the New Yam Festival, the Planting Festival, and the Harvest Festival. Like the women's dance, the Okonko dance could also be performed at any time during the village cultural events.

The women who participated in the event were dressed in their best uniforms. They wore their hair ties with black-and-white stripes and white blouses with colorful wrappers, which made them unique and attractive. Alice led the group and sang so beautifully. Her voice was very melodious. She and her group danced in a most stylish manner, attracting a lot of attention. They were surrounded by the crowd. Many people raised their heads to glance at them some more. The group entertained the crowd with many songs. When the songs ended, people were eager to hear some more, but the night has fallen.

Alice had much love for music and dance. During her youth, she had won several prizes in various local dance competitions. Performing wasn't new in her life. It was said that her performances in music and dance were the things that had won her husband's heart. As she thought about these things, she remembered that she'd had a bright future, but the death of her husband had brought her some setbacks. She'd wept bitterly on that fateful day when her former husband died. It hurt her so much because she had never had a child with him. Even now that she was married again, she still hadn't given birth to a child.

When the oracle or the village gods was consulted about her barrenness, she was told that in her first life, she'd had many children. Those children caused her a lot of trouble. When she couldn't bear the troubles anymore, she cursed her days and said, "I will never have any children of this nature that won't allow me to have rest of mine when I return into my next world." As it is said, the spirits are always alive to hear any evil utterance made by people and to take note of them. The oracle believed Alice had created the problem for herself because of being vocal. Therefore, she was told to cleanse the gods of the land with a male goat, a white fowl, twelve kola nuts, and two crocodile eggs before she could give birth again.

"Women who are endowed with the fruit of the womb do not have much value for them. It is only those like me who are denied the gift that have much value for children," Alice said to herself. She had done her part as a woman to conceive, but all she did proved unsuccessful. She began to consider whether to go and offer the sacrifice to the oracle or to remain childless and wait for the law of nature to take effect.

After the ceremony and the festivities were over, the two chiefs were finally led to their houses. Those who led Chief Udo to his house were entertained some more by the chief upon their arrival.

Chapter 6

THE GRADUATION CEREMONY

Udo's coronation as a chief made him even more famous. He was known throughout the entire village of Umueze. To maintain his titles and to display the hard work he had acquired before he was made chief, he began to contribute more to the development of his village. He was more generous to people than his colleague Ugo, and that made the villagers like him more.

He had promised to build corrugated shades in their village market on the day he was made chief, and he started at once to fulfill his promise. The construction was completed, and the newly renovated market square was handed over to the Umueze community. The market raised a better standard of trade in the village. Because of the new market, many villagers had a new job in their village.

Other neighboring villages came to the market to buy and sell their items to the Umueze village. The market raised a great deal of funds and brought new life to Umueze village. The individual traders made a great profit as well.

Many articles were sold, such as foodstuff, clothes, and farm products, including yams, cassava, onions, rice, beans, palm oil, and many others. Chief Udo sold his own yams in the market. Some of his food items were also sold in town where he made a lot of profits. When Alice saw that her husband's business needed more hands, she suspended her own trade and began to help her husband in selling the yams in their village market.

In his school, Chidi was in elementary six, and he was to take his final examination soon. He was still doing well in school. Before he reached elementary six, Chidi won an award for a quiz competition organized by the ministry of education to encourage academic excellence. His performance pleased his teachers and the headmaster of the school so much that they gave him some freewill gifts. Udo was so happy about his son's brilliant performance that he bought him a new shirt and a pair of trousers.

Later, Chidi took his final examination and the other subsidiary examinations set and marked by the school; the results were posted after a few weeks. As usual Chidi ranked first in the class.

The school scheduled a day to celebrate the graduation ceremony of the final-year students. The students' parents were invited to the event. On that day, the parents promptly arrived and took their seats. Chief Ugo was made the chairman of the event. On behalf of the school, Mr. Obi, the new school headmaster, gave a prize to Chidi for ranking as the first pupil in their school examinations.

The former headmaster of the school, Mr. Stephen, was on transfer to another school nearby. When Mr. Stephen was in Umueze Community School, he knew Chidi was an intelligent student and always commented on his good performance. On the day of the graduation, he went back to the school to witness the event.

Chief Ugo was called on to give some advice to the young boys and girls who were about to graduate from elementary six. During his speech, he congratulated the three best students for their brilliant performance. His best friend Chief Udo's son was among them. Although his son, Amona, wasn't in the top three, his performance was just as good for being in fourth position.

Chief Ugo wished them more success in their future academic pursuits and gave them some gifts. The school headmaster presented the school certificates to them.

Chidi and his father went home after the ceremony. Now that Chidi had finished elementary school, he was ready for his secondary school education.

"It seems that my dream about my son, Chidi, is becoming a reality. I hope God will continue to grant him success in all his school undertakings," Chief Udo said.

To celebrate his success in school, Alice prepared Chidi's favorite dish. Throughout that day, Udo and Alice made him happy. They wanted to encourage him to put more effort in his schoolwork since he would be attending secondary school in the future.

It was about this time that Chidi was maturing. Thus, he began to understand a little more about life. During this time, he heard that Alice wasn't his real mother. He had heard this first when he was six years in elementary school, but he'd been told that what he heard wasn't true. As a little child, he'd believed whatever his parents told him. Later, Chidi discovered the truth for himself when he saw the picture of a woman and his father in a drawer in their living room. He took the picture and kept it to himself. He decided to take the picture to his father to find out who the woman was. The woman in the picture somehow looked like him. That's why he wanted to find out.

Before Uloma's death, the picture had been kept on the table in the family living room. His father had removed it so Chidi wouldn't see it. He had been keeping the death of his mother a secret because the father believed that Chidi was still young to know. The picture had been misplaced when Udo was cleaning the house. He had looked for it but couldn't find it. He didn't bother to look for it anymore since Chidi was still too young to understand anything about his mother's death.

When Chidi came to him, Udo was relaxing in front of his house, where he usually stayed. He thought Chidi had a message from Alice.

"Excuse me, Father." Chidi approached him gently. "Who is this woman with you in this picture?" He brought out the picture at the same time.

"What picture? Where did you get that?" Udo asked. He was surprised and gazed at his son. He knew there was no need to hide what had been exposed to Chidi since he was now old enough to know about his mother's death.

"My son, there are no two ways about it. The woman you see in the picture is your real mother, but she is dead."

Udo felt sorry for Chidi, and he narrated the painful story of his deceased wife. "She died after giving you birth. The woman who is now living with us was present when everything took place. Your mother died because Alice couldn't revive her after all her efforts."

Chidi said, "Father, where were you when it happened?"

"I was at the farm. Nobody expected that she would give birth so soon. I returned at the point of her death." He paused and began again. "There was nothing to do to change the situation. She was already weak and calm, but Alice saved your life. After your mother was buried, Alice took you to the place where you were nursed to life.

"Then I married her so she could live with us and continue taking care of you, and you have seen her taking good care of you. As you can see, she has done a good job."

Chidi wept after hearing the story of his mother, but his father consoled him and persuaded him to forget everything. Chidi was happy because of Alice and everything she had done to nurture him from his childhood. They'd begun to live their lives as mother and child.

After a few days, Chidi received his school results; he would attend Obodo Grammar School, about ten kilometers away.

It will be difficult for Chidi to walk to his new school from home, his father thought. He began to consider whether the boy should live at school or go to school from home.

"But if he lives at school, no child would be living with me, but my wife. I need to stay close to him at all times," Udo said to himself.

After contemplating the situation, Udo decided his son should stay with him and attend the new school from home. Coincidentally, Chief Ugo's son was posted in the same school with Chidi. His father had decided to send his son to live at school where he could concentrate more on his studies.

When Chief Ugo learned Chief Udo's son would be going to the same school, he went to his friend to discuss the issue with him. Although Chief Udo had already decided not to allow his son to live at school, Chief Ugo discouraged the idea of traveling back and forth to school from home. Therefore, they decided that both boys would live at school.

Chapter 7

LIFE AT SCHOOL

Chidi and Amona were very glad on their first day of visiting the new school. They had come to be officially admitted. Before school reopened, their fathers had made their school uniforms. The newness of their uniforms made them look different from those of the other students. They found their way to school by following other students who traveled along the way.

Both walked majestically into the school premises. They had no experience of secondary school life, and perhaps because of that, they felt they would have the same liberties they'd had as primary school students. A group of boys, who were older than Chidi and his friend, approached the admissions office together with the new students. They were senior students from class five; even though they were older, they didn't dress neatly. They looked very rough. They were the older students who caused trouble in school. They were notorious in causing trouble among the younger students without the school authority's knowledge of their evil behavior.

The old students called Chidi and Amona. The boys moved reluctantly toward the students to answer their call, not knowing the amount of discipline required of them in this new environment. One of the senior students shouted at them, "Can't you run from there?"

"So you think you can do whatever you like in this school?" the shortest among them asked.

"No, senior," they almost answered at the same time.

"Who is your senior? Won't you answer, sir?" the fat one asked.

"We are sorry, sir," the new students frantically apologized. Amona began to sweat nervously.

"What is your name? I mean you, the black boy?" one of them asked.

"Amona is my name."

"Which primary school did you attend?"

"I went to Umueze Community School."

The same boy asked, "What about you?" He pointed at Chidi.

"I'm Chidi Udo. Both of us came from the same school," he added.

"So both of you are now attending the same school."

"Yes, sir," they answered.

"Now that you have come to this school, there are certain things you should not do as you used to do when you were in primary school. When you have completed your admission, the school principal will tell you more about that. Meanwhile, you must do whatever your seniors tell you to do; that's the first rule in this school.

"One of the other rules is that each newly admitted student should bring one Volkswagen to the senior students you met on your first day of school, which are me and my colleagues," the senior student explained.

The new boys were confused and wondered how they would purchase a Volkswagen car for each of the senior students. Chidi asked, "Sir, I don't understand what you mean by a Volkswagen. Are we to tell our fathers to buy a Volkswagen car for each of you?"

They laughed at them. "We don't mean Volkswagen cars. Volkswagen is the word used in this school to describe a big loaf of bread. Do you understand?"

"Yes, sir," they answered simultaneously.

"So when coming tomorrow, bring the bread with you," said the senior students.

After Chidi and Amona finished talking with them, they quickly went to the admissions office to get registered. They had wasted a lot of time talking with the senior students. Consequently, they couldn't complete their admission on that day and had to come back the following day.

The next day, Chief Ugo joined them to help expedite their admission. Chief Udo would have come, but he had to supervise the laborers working on his farm. Chief Ugo took over the duty to pay all their school fees. Later, they moved from their house to live in the school.

While they were at school, their fathers often visited them with food and money. Chidi and Amona began to learn the secondary school life. They started to participate in such school activities as going to the stream to fetch water and getting involved in the morning chores and prayers.

Apparently, Chidi and Amona had forgotten what the senior students had told them to bring on their first day of school. One day they saw the Senior students when they were on their way to the stream to fetch some water. At the last hostel, one of the students confronted them.

"Hey! You two!" he called out in a loud voice. Chidi and Amona stopped to see who was calling them. When Chidi saw the boy, he remembered him, but Amona didn't recognize him until he came to meet them.

"Aren't you Chidi and Amona?" one of the senior students asked.

"We are!" they answered.

"Why didn't you come back to see us as we had agreed?"

"We came back the following day to meet you, but you were gone."

"Gone where?" the tall student asked.

"We didn't know where you went," Amona answered.

"I hope you have the Volkswagen now," the other student said.

"Yes," Chidi answered.

"Okay, I see that you are going to the stream. After you get back from the stream, meet us back here. Do you hear me?" the tall student among them asked.

"Yes, sir," the new students answered.

"If you fail to come back, I will get you," the older student added.

After returning from the stream, the new students came back to see them as they had promised. The village school had no running water. Students usually got their daily water from the spring near the school. When they returned, they were lucky that they had two loaves of bread, which their fathers had brought to them on their last visit. They gave one loaf to the older students.

As they came into their hostel, they were surprised to see one of the older students waiting for them. The other senior student thought the new students might not come back; he had gone to look for them.

"You are welcome once again in the students' forum," they said to the new students as they walked with the student into their dormitory room. "Where are the Volkswagens?" they asked.

The word *Volkswagen* was no longer a new language to them. They knew exactly what the senior students were talking about.

"We came with one loaf of bread, the only bread our father had given us to give you," said Chidi.

"Did you tell your father that we requested bread from you? Is that what you did?" the big student screamed. Suddenly, he was afraid their deal might have been exposed because what they had requested from the new students was illegal.

"No, we didn't tell our fathers. If we have told them, they would have come to the school to find out."

"What did you tell them?"

"Nothing! Nothing at all," Amona answered.

"Okay, start to go back to your dormitory. If you tell your parents about this, you'll be in hot soup—I mean, in trouble," the tall student warned. As they were told, Chidi and Amona quickly left them and went back to their room after the student had taken the bread from them.

Chapter 8

THE NEW YAM FESTIVAL

Back in Umueze, the New Yam Festival was a seasonal occasion. Traditionally, it was the period when sons and daughters of Umueze gathered to celebrate their newly harvested yams. In addition, the indigenous of the village who lived in the other parts of the world returned home for the celebration.

Other villagers also celebrated the New Yam Festival, but the festival in Umueze was considered the most outstanding and well celebrated.

Two weeks before the festival, the villagers started to prepare for the event. Individual families went to their farms to get food, and firewood was stockpiled. Chief Udo and his family would normally participate as well. The festival was a three-day event. During the three days, any villager was prohibited to go to a farm; it was a holiday for the village. Everyone had to stock up on food and firewood in advance for the festival.

One of the things that marked the festival was the

wealth competition between the village chiefs. In this case, the village chiefs would showcase how rich and famous they were by purchasing expensive items for the occasion, which would make their names the talk of the town. The newly crowned chiefs Udo and Mazi Ugo bought two large cows to be slaughtered.

Another important preparation was the way individual houses were decorated. The walls of the mud houses were plastered with red soil. Charcoal and white powder were used to further decorate the walls. The women of the village made different kinds of artistic designs on the walls of their houses. In addition, the young men replaced the roofs of the house with new raffia palm leaves. The entire village was kept neat and ready for the occasion.

On the first day, everyone was ready for the festival. The women washed their mortar and pestles and began to grind their melon, which was one of the special foods offered to the visitors. The melon was mixed with pepper, onions, salt, and spices. Very early in the morning, the town crier would blow the village elephant horn to alert every one of the event.

The elephant horn would serve as a reminder to all the villagers that D day had come. The horn plays an important role in the history of Umueze. Someone recorded that the founder of Umueze had killed an elephant terrorizing the entire village. After sharing the meat among his family, he gave his first son the animal's horn to keep as a remembrance. Thus, whenever any occasion was to take place in Umueze, the horn would first be blared to alert the people.

Before midday, the village square had already filled with people. The village masquerades and other activities had taken over. The special food prepared had been set aside. Two large cows were slaughtered and cooked. The food was placed on the tables for people to enjoy.

As the chiefs and their guests enjoyed themselves in the king's palace, others were in their various houses, celebrating, as well. Each family would prepare their own food. Some would kill chickens; others would kill ducks to prepare their food. The first two days of the festival were celebrated at individuals' homes, and everything went well.

The third day of the festival was celebrated in the most exciting way. It was the day the "King of Yams" title would be awarded to the best yam producer of the year. During the previous year, Chief Udo had won the title. The title attracted a lot of prizes and honor. The person who received it would have to be at least twenty-five years old; his barn had to be filled with yams, and the person must also be known in the village to be a good person. If the best yam producer's neighbors didn't consider him to be a good person, he wouldn't receive the title.

The title made a lot of people, especially the men,

to work hard to produce food for the village. It was a big challenge for every man in Umueze. In the village square, which was the usual venue for the occasion, people began to gather with curiosity to learn who would win the title for the year. Before the title could be awarded, the village cabinet, composed of the king as the supreme head and the elders in council, had to meet to select the winner. The council had already taken a week to examine the contestants.

After some time, the king and some of the elders went to the village square. The traditional dancers, who had been entertaining the crowd, ceased their dance abruptly, as a mark of respect to the king, as he entered the crowd. The King of yam title wasn't regarded as the chieftaincy title; it could be given only to people in the village square, not in the king's palace

Based on the procedures, the king rose from his seat and admonished the people. He called three names of people who had done well. These people were Atako, Ani, and Idowu. But the best among them was Idowu, so he was declared the winner for the year. When the declaration was made, there was big jubilation from the crowd. But there were some people who didn't agree with the decision. Some were friends and relatives of the two men who had lost the contest.

They murmured that the king and his council had done an injustice.

A leader of the people is always the subject of

caricature; his decisions are subject to silent oppositions. Some will like him while others may hate him. After the ceremony, those unhappy with the decision incited Atako and Ani to take up the matter against the king and his cabinet to the village court. They did as they were advised; they took the matter to the village customary court.

Atako was known in Umueze as a stubborn human being; besides his stubbornness, it was certain that he was a hard-working farmer. He would have won the title had it not been for his personal character. The decision made at the contest was also based on individual character, which Atako had failed.

Ani encouraged him to sue the king and his council. Ani knew quite well that he wouldn't have won the contest; he believed Atako had a better chance than him, if the decision at the contest had been done right.

On the day the case was to be heard in court, the chiefs and elders of Umueze assembled in the village square next to the king's palace. This was the place where cases involving the villagers were decided. Atako was called on to make a statement before the people. He stood up and said, "After the King of the Yam contest was awarded to Idowu, I came to realize that the decision was wrong and unfair. I believed I was cheated. When the village judges first came to my barn to assess the quality of my handwork, like they did to other farmers, they didn't find any fault in my barn. The barn was full of quality yams, which was required to win the contest, so I don't see the reason why I should lose the title. I believe the king and his council have done an injustice to me."

In a case like this, the two parties involved are allowed to present their cases before the court; then, from their statements a judgment is determined. One of the council members was given a chance to defend Atako's statement.

"Atako has made big mistake by declaring himself the winner of the contest; as it is said, a pot shouldn't decide the kind of soap that should be used in cleaning its dirt, rather than the owner of the pot. The title doesn't belong to any of the contestant. The contestants are our guests, and we are the host. The guests have no right or privilege to make decisions on this matter. It is only the hosts who make decisions on the contest. We didn't do an injustice to anyone. Our decisions were based on the rules of the contest. Idowu has the right to the title because he merited it, and our decision was unanimous. Atako decided for himself to be the winner of the contest and forgot that the decision was made by the four judges."

The cabinets met for two weeks before the winner of the title was decided.

"Your petition in this court, as I can see it, has no merit," the speaker for the council said. He further told Atako that it was his stubbornness that had caused him the title. "If you deserve such an award, you must change your behavior. Accusing the king and his council of injustice was clear evidence of disrespect to the king, the council, and the community at large.

"According to the traditions of the village, the titles can be awarded only to a person who has respect for the elders, the chiefs, the king, and the councils. Therefore, with two counts against you, you are to pay the sum of fifty shillings to the court for false accusations against the king and his council. In addition, you should apologize to them for the insult."

That was how Atako lost the case and paid the village customary court the fine.

Chapter 9

A DAY OF SORROW

The case Atako lost wounded his spirit, and he was very angry. He felt he'd been denied justice. To avenge the loss, he pondered what he would do to have revenge on the village.

Ikpeama was a place of safety and freedom. It was a village not far from Umueze. When someone commits an evil on his or her own land, such a person often runs to Ikpeama to take refuge. As long as the person isn't caught before he or she reaches the village, the person becomes free from punishment or retaliation.

The village was known to be the land of refuge. Ikpeama, the land of freedom, began to protect people in the early days when villages used to engage in tribal war. Whenever anyone or people ran away from their village to Ikpeama, the king of the village absolutely protected such people from being killed. The same protection was given to anyone who did evil and ran into the land.

Atako was a hunter and farmer. He would leave his house every night for hunting and return the following day. When he left his house one night, no one knew what was in his mind. He planned to set the village barn on fire while everyone was asleep. The task didn't take long; the village barns were destroyed.

The villagers began to look for the person who had done this evil to them. They thought it was an outsider until they found out an insider had committed that evil, and that insider turned to be Atako. The village Age Grades, the security people who watched and protected the village and their belongings, were sent to Atako's grandfather, Ikoro to find out whether he was the one who had set their barns on fire. The age grades in Umueze village are the group of men that were born in the same year or one year apart. These men are selected by the village to run the affairs of the village including protecting the security of the community. They are the village law enforcements agent. When the Age Grade came to Ikoro, he confirmed that Atako had set the village barn on fire.

"It is unwise to inquire about the taste of a stool, because from the smell, someone should know how awful it would taste." His grandfather described Atako's awful behavior using a parable.

"Everyone knows Atako well as a stubborn and difficult man. His bad behavior had made everyone believe he was the person who set the village barn on fire. After the village Age Grade went to his house and couldn't find him, they went to his grandfather, Mazi-Ikoro to inquire from him." It was Ikoro who told the Age Grade that Atako had escaped to Ikpeama for his safety.

"He quickly came to my house, took some of his belongings, and ran away. I didn't know why he was in such a hurry. When I asked him what was happening to him, he said nothing to me," Ikoro explained.

After the Age Grade reported the message they had received from Ikoro to the king and his council, everybody became aware that Atako, who had escaped to Ikpeama, had set the fire.

Atako had left a curse for himself, his family, and relatives. An unscrupulous and heartless human being destroyed the village barn, which had taken several years of hard labor to build. In retaliation, the angry villagers demolished his house. His fellow villagers wanted to kill him for the evil he had done to them. Now the villagers had to start life all over again. Their forefathers often said, "When a fowl defecates on the ground, it will leave the ground and perch on a bamboo tree."

Atako had polluted his village and gone to live in another one. Perhaps one day he might do the same thing to the people whom he had gone to live with. Sometimes it is hard for someone to change a bad habit in old age. Who knows what Atako might do again? Atako was notorious and stubborn; it was only his stubbornness that would bring him to an end. The village had wanted him dead, but his grandfather didn't want him to die. He had wished him to live and face the consequences of the crime he had committed.

"I wish Atako a life sentence, not death. If he dies, his evil will die with him, but if he lives, he will live to pay for his evil deed," Mazi-Ikoro advised.

It took the Umueze villagers twelve years to heal the wound inflicted on them in one day. Those twelve years were a period of famine and suffering. People from nearby villages sent food to Umueze Village to support them. Unfortunately, some died because of famine.

Someone once said, "Any sickness that has a cure must also be endured." The people of Umueze had suffered enough, so they began to find solutions to the problems of their land. People from nearby villages gave some free seed yams and other food crops to be planted in Umueze farms, which had helped to improve their lives. Twelve years later, their lives were brought back to normal, but their barns weren't the same again. The only barn that survived the burning was Chief Udo's barn because his barn was not located in the same place like other villagers' barns.

Atako lived for one year in Ikpeama with no relatives or wife. At this time, he started to regret his evil deed. He began to feel the absence of his village and family. He felt lonely in the new place where he had come to live. After he lived in Ikpeama for two years, his wife and two children came to live with him. After this, his life gradually began to change for the better, but his life couldn't be the same as it was. Atako had gone to Ikpeama with great wealth, and the people had welcomed him to live with them. They gave him freedom. The king of the village gave him a house to live with his family.

Atako couldn't return to Umueze after he destroyed their barn. In his lonesome moments, he cried in silence, "My iniquities against my village have made me to become a fugitive. If I should return, they would kill me. I have become an enemy to my own people.

"A child cannot be older than his parents. I was angered. I took action without thought, and now the consequences of my actions are upon me. If I couldn't go back home, then I would live forever in another man's land."

Atako couldn't return to his village because of the evil he had done to his people. He regretted his actions. He wished he could be given a second chance.

He later died and was buried in Ikpeama.

Chapter 10

THE CLEANSING SACRIFICE

After Chidi went to live at school, Chief Udo and his wife were left alone in the house. After remaining childless for so long, Alice went and brought her nephew to live with them to fill the vacuum Chidi had created. Even though her nephew came to live with them, that didn't stop Alice from worrying too much about her childless condition. Her worries became so obvious that her husband began to take notice.

Early one morning, the village was very dark. There was no visibility. The cock crowed for the first time, which meant the daylight hadn't appeared yet. Alice decided to go and make the sacrifice to the oracle. Her husband had bought the things needed for the sacrifice.

The journey that leads to success requires determination, courage, patience, and hard work. Even though Alice met ghosts, the night bird, and other dangerous animals on her way to the forest, she was determined to do whatever it took to have a child.

Chief Udo was fast asleep when his wife left on her journey. Suddenly, he got up from the bed; he looked around the house, but he couldn't find his wife. Next, he took out his machete and followed the direction of his wife's footprints.

He headed toward the evil forest. As he moved farther, he heard the cry of the goat Alice had taken with her. Before he could reach his wife, she was already at the middle of the forest, where the oracle was erected.

The evil forest was always quiet. Anyone who entered it would mistakenly be devoured by pythons. There were three oracles in the forest. Each of them had its own responsibility. They possessed frightening features that made those who came to visit them be afraid. Thick smoke came out of their mouths. Where they sat was strange and wonderful. It was believed that anyone who went to the gods with any kind of illness or barrenness would find healing in the smoke.

Udo hid out of Alice's sight when she performed the sacrifice. She took the male goat, tied it before the oracle, and brought forth the other things required. She stood by the oracle and watched with high concentration to those things she placed before the oracle. As she watched the sacrifice, the thick smoke began to change into flames, which later engulfed all the sacrifices placed before the oracle: the goat, the white fowl, the three crocodile eggs, and the kola nut. The fire consumed all of them.

When the sacrifice was over, Alice turned back in the direction of the village and headed home slowly without turning back until she reached home. Her husband followed her at a distance to ensure she returned home safely.

Once she returned home, she began to regain her normal disposition. She was happy about paying the debt she owed to the spirits and the ancestors. Since she had settled with the gods, she began to hope that she would bear a child someday. After returning from the forest, she cleared her mind that she had nothing to fear anymore.

Two years had gone by, and Alice hadn't become pregnant. Udo worried more than Alice did. His wife's barrenness didn't annoy him, but her decision to go against his faith did. He didn't believe the oracle could bring a solution to the problem. But what people had said, coupled with his wife's pressure on him, had made him buy those things needed for the sacrifice. Now, two years had passed since the sacrifice, and still Alice hadn't conceived. "I shall be a fool if what I have suffered for doesn't come through," she said.

Finally, Alice just reached forty-five when she conceived and gave birth to a baby girl, whom she named Ogechi, which means "God's time." Many who knew her age and how much she had suffered couldn't believe such an old woman could give birth to a child. However, some said her sacrifice to the oracles had made her conceive.

Everyone had his or her opinion about her pregnancy. Some believe everybody has his or her time God has appointed to him or her. Hence, it was appointed that Alice would have a female child at the age of forty-five. Although she was ignorant of her destiny, in her effort to have her way, she went against the will of God. Alice moved faster than her destiny. The pressure was too great; her age wasn't on her side. She decided to follow the traditions and beliefs of the village. She had to spend her money and time, and she took the lonely road to the oracle to have a child.

Alice believed her effort was a success. Others had believed it wasn't her time yet to have a baby. Chief Udo was so glad Alice had finally born a child. They decided to celebrate the birth of the baby. All the parents in the village brought their children to Chief Udo's house to celebrate the birth of their newborn. The celebration was organized for the children. They prepared all kinds of food.

It was the belief of the people that children pave the way for unborn babies to come into the world. The people also believed the celebration helped to preserve the lives of newborn babies. All the children danced around the baby as she looked at them from her bed.

The children smiled at her as they sang and dancing around her. With their song, they told the baby she was welcome. Everyone sang and wished the family the best.

Ogechi brought joy and happiness to her mother, who had suffered for many years, hoping to have a child. Now, if Alice couldn't bear another child, it wouldn't matter anymore because she was no longer called a barren woman. She was known in the village as the woman who gave birth in her later years.

Chapter 11

THE DEATH OF CHIEF UDO

Chidi was very intelligent in elementary school, and he gained a lot of admiration and respect for his smarts. His most remarkable achievement was winning first prize for an essay competition held at the time he was in elementary four. His fellow students nicknamed him "Academic Wizard"; even his teachers knew him by that name.

In his second year in high school, Chidi began to consider attending a university. His father had left no stone unturned to ensure his son completed his education at the highest level he wished. He paid his son's school fees and supplied provisions whenever they were needed.

Unfortunately for Chidi, his father died when all hope for surviving and continuing in school depended on him. A hunter mistook him for an antelope in the forest and instantly shot him dead. Chief Udo's remains were taken to the hospital and kept in a mortuary. Not everybody knew he was dead. Instead, the people were told he was unconscious.

As it is said, "Bad news travels faster than a warring arrow." Later, the hidden truth was exposed. Chidi received the news at school, and he was uncontrollable; he fell to the ground and wept bitterly, lamenting in different voices nobody could understand. He almost became insane, but his friends were able to console him in the end.

Chidi later realized no amount of weeping could bring his father back to life. He was brought home with Amona and some other students. Some of their teachers came along to sympathize with him.

As difficult as it was to control Chidi at school, the death was also difficult for Alice, who was at home.

Her husband's death appeared to be a bad omen. This was the second time her husband had died. Apparently, Alice had bad luck in her marriage. Her first husband had died when she had just been married; now her second husband had died too. Udo's death was a big loss. Now she would have to start her life over again with a twelve-month-old baby.

Chidi, motherless since birth, had become fatherless, too. Now he felt there was no hope of survival for him. He wondered what his future would be like in the absence of his father. Friends and relatives came to comfort him. Some people, like Chief Ugo, promised to see that he finished his secondary school.

In a situation like Chidi's, it was common for people to offer assistance, but the question was, how true were their promises?

There was a custom of the people when a person killed another personal unknowingly; the accuser must swear before the village oracle and confess that the killing was an accident. If his or her confession was untrue, the person would die a mysterious death. Many believed the gods of the land would avenge the person killed. So the man who had shot Chief Udo was brought to the village oracle, where he was made to confess. His name was Ezechi, the hunter.

Chief Udo had been a famous man when he was alive. He had done many great things to develop his village. His death was a great loss to the people of Umueze, so they decided to give him an honorable burial. It would require large sums of money in keeping with the honor intended.

There was a man named Ike who lived in the same village as Chief Udo. When he was alive, no one actually knew him as a relative to Chief Udo; neither had he done anything for the welfare of his family. After Chief Udo died, the man came to claim he was a relative of Chief Udo. He took over Udo's burial arrangement and was in charge of everything concerning the burial.

He made a large withdrawal of money from Chief Udo's account that would be used for the burial. During the burial, Ike bought two goats, one cow, fifty pots of palm wine, and three bags of rice, cassava flour, kola nuts, and other foodstuff. In addition, he hired a musical group from the town to provide entertainment. All the burial expenses came from late Chief Udo' savings, the money Udo had saved for Chidi's college education.

The chief's body was laid to rest after the burial events to honor him were over. The burial had consumed almost all the money Chief Udo had saved while he was alive. Afterward, there was no money left for food or school expenses for Chidi. The family was left to suffer.

Ike wasn't seen after the funeral was over. He spent a lot of money on the burial and he also took some of the money for himself. When he was called on to explain the burial expenses to Udo's wife, he couldn't give an accurate account of the money.

Chief Ugo did the best he could, as a friend to late Chief Udo, to help his son. He sent Chidi back to school to complete his education as he had promised.

Two years later, Chidi finished his secondary school, but there was no money for his college education. In the circumstances where he found himself, all he could do was find some kind of work to do. Thus, he did all kinds of odd jobs in the village just to survive.

During the farming season, when farms were clearing and cultivating the land, some farmers would hire him to do some work for them. At the end of the

Chapter 12

THE LIFE OF CHIDI AFTER HIS FATHER'S DEATH

At the end of the year when people who lived in the township had come home, Chidi was taken to the town to live with one of the village men named Okoro. Chief Ugo had introduced Chidi to the man. Chief Ugo remembered the plan Chief Udo had had for his son. Even when his first wife died, Udo had done all he could to train him. He had never dreamed that his son would suffer. But now that he had died, his dreams were no more.

Chidi had suffered a lot in the village. That was the reason Chief Ugo went to Okoro to tell him about the boy's plight. After Mazi Ugo and Okoro discussed his situation, Okoro agreed to take Chidi to the city to live with him and to train him to be a trader.

Okoro was a trader who had lived in the township for more than ten years. He knew everything about township life. He sold clothes for a living, and when

Chidi came to live with him, he sold clothes, too. He was a hard-working boy. It didn't take him long to sell all the clothes he took to the market. He went to all the streets to sell the clothes his master has given him to sell.

One day, as he was selling clothes illegally along the road, the police caught and detained him. This happened while his master was out of town. Chidi was held in police custody for two weeks, and he was finally released after his master had paid the sum of eighty shillings.

After his release, his master was angry with him for having to spend the money for his release. That made his master to mistreat him, even to starve him for many days as a sort of punishment. When Chidi couldn't bear the mistreatment anymore, he escaped as he went to sell clothes as usual. With money he made from selling clothes, he took a train to another town.

He waited a long time for the train to come. After waiting so long, he contemplated whether to go back home to his master. But he was afraid his master might increase his punishment for returning late. Perhaps this time he might even beat him up.

Mr. Okoro was a mean person. His harsh treatment to his servants had made two of his boys leave his house. Chidi had started to suffer the same treatment that had caused the other servants to leave his house.

While he waited for the train, many other

passengers began to arrive at the station. About five yards from where he was sitting; there was a man who didn't sit down like every other passenger, even though there were available seats. The man was busy reading a newspaper when he tried to put some money in his pocket, but he missed the target, and the money fell on the ground. Perhaps no one saw when the money fell, but Chidi saw it all.

He moved from his seat and went to the man. "Excuse me, sir. Your money fell on the ground," he said to the man. The man came back to himself and picked up the money. He continued reading his newspaper without making any effort to say thank you. But all the same, his behavior didn't mean he didn't appreciate Chidi's kindness. Instead he was so busy reading his newspaper with much interest that he couldn't have the chance to say thanks.

But in his mind, he couldn't believe the boy would be honest enough to do what he'd done. Especially in these days, young people are no longer trusted. The man thought Chidi must have come from a good family. A few minutes after the incident, the train approached the station. The conductor checked all the tickets. Those who had a lot of luggage paid their luggage fare. Once everyone had boarded the train, the train sounded its horn and began to move along the rail. The heavy vibration of the engine made everything in the train shake vigorously, including the passengers.

The journey lasted so long that everyone became tired. Some even fell asleep. Chidi leaned on the back seat. Other passengers sat on both sides of him. He didn't sleep, but sometimes he closed his eyes after straining for so long since he was just looking through the window as the train moved along. When the train approached nearby bushes, he started to see trees as if they were running very fast. Chidi could easily notice when the train moved at its highest speed because of the movement of the trees.

Among those sitting beside him was a fat woman who had been sleeping all the time. It seemed as though she had taken a sleeping pill before she entered the train. About two kilometers from the first station stop, the train blew its horn. Those who were to leave the train were to get ready to leave. That was the precise time the woman woke up from her sleep. She rose with her clothes on her lap and began to search earnestly for something. No one knew what she was looking for when she couldn't find it. In madness, she turned to Chidi, who sat beside her, and asked, "Boy, did you see my purse?"

He shook his head.

The woman didn't believe Chidi, so she continued to question him. "What are you telling me? You mean, you didn't see my purse that I placed on my lap?" she asked more loudly.

Chidi was confused and couldn't say anything. The situation attracted the attention of the other passengers, who started to put pressure on him. A similar event had taken place recently on the train when someone snatched a woman's handbag from her. The passengers thought Chidi could be one of those thieves. They were about to put pressure on him to produce the purse when the man who sat at the opposite end intervened for him.

"Please do not touch that boy. He is innocent; he is not in possession of the purse. You better search for it carefully," the man exclaimed. It was the man Chidi had helped recover his money at the train station.

Everyone looked at the man as he began to narrate his story to the angry passengers. He explained that Chidi had helped him recovered the money that fell from his pocket. Therefore, he testified that Chidi must be innocent.

The story made the passengers restrain their anger. Some joined to look for the purse elsewhere. Finally, someone found the purse between the two seats where Chidi and the woman were sitting. Perhaps if the man hadn't intervened for Chidi, the passengers would have beaten him up. Even worse, they could have either killed him or handed him over to the police. Then who would have come to Chidi's rescue? That probably would have been the end of his life. The woman later apologized to Chidi.

At last, the train came to its destination. Chidi had to spend all night in the station because he wanted to join another train that would take him to a nearby town. It was a terrible night for Chidi since the mosquitoes wouldn't permit him to sleep. He was restless and uncomfortable throughout the night. He could easily hear the mosquitoes as they hovered around his ears. In the morning, he noticed that his entire body was swollen with mosquito bites. Very early that morning, he joined another train that would take him to another township.

The journey was an overnight one. He thought about stopping at a nearby town, but when he arrived there, he changed his mind and decided to stay on the train until the last stop. He had nothing with him except the little money left after he had paid his fare.

From the railway station, where the train had stopped, he traveled to the east. After a while, he was hot and exhausted. There was no one around. He felt a horrible loneliness. He came to a certain street; there were white houses with wooden doors. He noticed the ground was covered with a powdery-gray dust that had drifted into heaps up to a foot high. As the night was fast approaching, he began to remember the terrible night he'd had in the station with the mosquitoes. Although a few insects had started to hunt around him, sticking to his hair and the sweat on his face, insects weren't as plentiful in this place as they were at the railway station.

He came to a certain hotel and sat on the sidewalk. He was extremely tired. His legs were hurting him, and he was getting hungry at the moment.

The hotel was a two-story building in British colonial style with an iron gate. Chidi had spent most of the money he had on his way. There was no hope of surviving his immediate condition. After some time at the gate, he began to observe a figure of somebody coming toward the hotel. As the image drew closer, he noticed it was a gentleman in a black suit. He was afraid to talk to the man; the man's appearance intimidated him. His conscience told him not to approach the man. Chidi was in a battle with his mind as the man was about to walk past the gate.

Chidi mustered the courage to say something. "Excuse me, sir." The man looked at him as he spoke.

"Who are you?" the man asked in a sonorous voice, which frightened him.

"I'm Chidi Udo, the son of Chief Udo of Umueze," he stammered.

The word *chief* caught the man's attention, since he thought the boy must have come from a noble family. "What can I do for you?" the man asked.

"Sir, I am a stranger here. I do not know where to go; I don't know anyone around here. I have come all the way from the village to look for a job. I came to this township yesterday by train, and I do not have any money left with me. Now I am stranded and hungry. Please, sir, would you mind giving me some money to buy some food."

The man had pity on him. He took him to a nearby restaurant in the hotel and bought Chidi something to eat. Chidi ate satisfactorily and regained his strength.

The man's name was Jack Williams, an American. He had recently come to live in Africa to do business. He had just arrived two months ago and was looking for someone who would live with him and help him in taking care of his domestic work. He'd found Chidi at the right time.

"Would you like to stay with me?" the man asked.

Chidi nodded. "Yes, sir, I would."

Mr. Williams had a well-furnished house in one of the estates in town.

That was where he'd been living since he arrived, and he would be staying there until he completed his duty, which would take him more than three years or more. That night he had come to the hotel to have some refreshment, as he usually did sometimes.

It seems that God had granted Chidi the opportunity for a better life in his journey of no destination. Because of mistreatment, he was forced to look for a better life for himself. He was determined to die and meet his Father if he failed to survive.

Mr. Williams told Chidi to wait in the restaurant. He had nothing with him except the shirt and trouser he wore that night, which were covered with dust. He waited patiently at the restaurant. It took Mr. Williams quite some time to finish his drinks. Chidi had waited so long and was tired. He was about to doze off when Mr. Williams came out of the bar to make a phone call. Perhaps he forgot about Chidi until he saw him sitting at the place where he'd left him. He remembered and called him.

"Boy! Where are you?"

Chidi quickly woke up and regained his consciousness. "Sir, I am here," he responded. He got up quickly and followed him. Mr. Williams had parked his car on the other side of the hotel. Chidi followed him reluctantly, as if he wasn't willing to go with him. Frankly, he was as happy as someone who had just won the lottery. At the moment, it was already nighttime, and there was no visible light outside the hotel.

Chidi became afraid as they moved along in the dark. Mr. Williams approached his car, took his key, and opened the door. "Boy, go to the other side." He motioned to Chidi, who moved with fear. He didn't know exactly how to open the car door.

"Pull the handle backward," Mr. Williams instructed.

Chidi pulled the handle, opened the door, and got

in the car. It was the first time he had been in anyone's car. He was almost afraid to enter it.

Gradually, they drove away from the hotel and moved toward the road that led to the east side, where Mr. Williams lived. Chidi was busy staring at the nice buildings and the advertisements, especially those lit by fluorescent lights. They finally came to the man's house.

Mr. Williams wanted to know more about Chidi, so he probed him with some questions. "Is your father a chief in your village?"

"Yes," Chidi answered. "He was."

Mr. Williams began to wonder why the son of a village chief should be stranded and hungry in the street. "Tell me, Chidi, what about your father and mother?"

"My father and mother have died," he told him.

"I'm so sorry to hear that. Was it an accident?" Mr. Williams asked.

"No, sir. My mother died when I was born, and my father later died while I was in school. He was accidentally shot to death in the bush by a hunter who thought he was an antelope. After the death of my father, I came to the city to live with a man from my village. The man abused and mistreated me so much that I decide to run away for my life. That's how I came to the city and eventually met you at the hotel gate."

Mr. Williams felt sorry for him and promised him

he would help him. After Chidi had arrived in his new home, he began to have a better life. His new boss gave him a lot of privileges. He performed all the domestic work with diligence; he was good in all aspects of the jobs he'd been given to do. His boss began to like and respect him for the job he performed. Chidi had worked so hard when he was living with Okoro with no sign of hope. But since he came to Mr. Williams's house, there was a sign of hope on the horizon, unlike his former boss, who had mistreated and abused him.

After living with him for a year, Mr. Williams discovered that Chidi could do better in other aspects of work besides domestic work. Jack, who had come to Africa to establish fabric industry, had completed the business. After the industry was established, there weren't enough employees to fill all the positions, so Mr. Williams decided to employ Chidi to work full-time at the factory.

Now, after Chidi had lived with Mr. Williams for two years, Mr. Williams felt that Chidi had matured enough to live on his own.

Before Mr. Williams became a business man, he'd been a college professor in America. He used to teach humanities. He believed every human being was born with two things: strong and weak potentials. All human potentials complement each other. Strong potentials are those areas where people do best during their lifetimes; the weak potentials are those areas where people tend to slack during their lifetimes. He saw those areas in Chidi and came to believe Chidi had more strong potentials than weak ones and that he should be given a chance to use those. He believed Chidi would do well when given the opportunity.

He decided to give Chidi the opportunity to live on his own. He helped him find another place to live and furnished it for him. After working in the business for a couple of years, Chidi gained a lot of experience, which made his boss promote him to manager. He was given a company car to run the business. Chidi had become an independent man. He was making a good salary for his work and began to enjoy life.

Now that he had some money, he started to remember his village; his late father's friend Chief Ugo; and his stepmother, Alice. He wrote a letter to Alice and informed her that he was still alive. Alice couldn't believe it because when Chidi had run away from Okoro's house, people from the village had been sent to the town to look for him. They'd looked for him throughout the entire town and couldn't see him. Later, everybody gave up, forgot all about him, and thought he was dead. Alice had grieved so much about him.

It was a surprise and a happy moment for Alice when she received a message from Chidi that he was still alive and would be visiting home at the end of the year.

When she received the message, she went to Chief Ugo and informed him. Chief Ugo couldn't believe the news either. They waited for the day when Chidi would come to the village. Since the death of Chief Udo, Alice had suffered so much; she'd decided to go back to her old trade. That was how she took care of herself and her daughter, who was now seven years old. There was no money to send her to school. The little money they had was just enough to buy food.

Chidi couldn't go home at the end of the year as he had promised because of so much work. He had to reschedule his trip for the following year. He wrote back to Alice to inform her about the changes he had made to his trip back home.

Chidi was somebody who was always sincere with himself and others. He didn't like to spoil his name. He remembered the clothes he had taken with him when he ran away from Okoro's house because of the abuse he'd suffered. He offered to pay him back for the clothes when he returned home. He believed that a good name is better than silver and gold.

Chapter 13

CHIDI RETURNS TO HIS VILLAGE

As he had promised his people, Chidi returned home at the end of the year. They celebrated his arrival. People who used to live in the same compound with Chidi and his father came out of their houses to welcome him. As he was walking into the compound, he started to remember his father's compound and the changes that had taken place all those years, especially to his father's house. Chidi noticed that the village was no longer what it used to be. The houses were very old, including his father's. The roof, the walls, and the corridors had worn out completely. The only part of the house that was still intact was the room where his father and his wife used to live. But at the moment, Alice and her daughter were living in that room.

A young girl and her mother came out of the house, greeted him, and took his luggage into the house. They were Alice and Ogechi. There was a new white car parked in front of their compound, Chidi's vehicle. Everybody in the village came out to see his new car. They were surprised to see that Chidi's life had changed for good.

Chidi still recognized Alice and her daughter despite their age. Alice's face had begun to shrink a little. Ogechi had started to reach the age of maturity. Her mother had told her earlier that her brother would be coming home that day. Both mother and child were anxiously waiting for him to arrive. As soon as Chidi walked into the compound, Ogechi ran ahead of her mother to welcome him. Alice and her daughter both hugged him and walked with him into their house.

Chidi was the only son of Umueze who had returned home from town with a new vehicle. His presence in the village was noticed. People from other compounds came to his father's house just to see him.

Some of the people who visited him had told him they were related to his father and his late mother, Uloma. Chidi had started to wonder where these newly discovered relatives were living when his father and mother died. He remembered how hard it was to go to sleep sometimes without food. Nobody claimed him as a relative. Now that his life had changed for the good, everybody had become his relative. Without hesitation, Chidi was still generous to those who came to see him; to some of them he gave gifts. To those who didn't receive many gifts during his visit, he promised to give them something more on his next visit.

Chidi couldn't believe the so-called relatives who couldn't help to fix his father's crumbling house while he was gone or to help weed the grass in the compound. Some parts of the house's walls had started to fall in due to rainfall. No one had cared for the house, even when his father had died; those who had turned out for his burial only came to squander his wealth. After the burial was over, nobody was seen again. The poor widow, her daughter, and Chidi were left to suffer in the village. In order to find a better life, Chidi had gone to live with a non-relative in town. One day after he had gone to sale clothes for his boss, he never returns home. After he could not be found, he was declared lost. At the time he was lost, the newly discovered relatives that are hovering around him now, did not come to look for him.

Now that Chidi had acquired some wealth, everyone had come to claim him as his or her relative. Some came to see what they could get from him. Chidi believed these were the same people who had spent his father's wealth when he died; now that he had returned to the village with some money, they returned to visit him. These people hadn't looked for him while he had gone, but they had come to visit him now that he had become successful.

In all the previous years he had suffered, no one had claimed ownership of Chidi. *What a wicked world where someone can be claimed only when he or she becomes successful; however, the same person would be rejected if he or she fails to succeed*, Chidi thought.

When Chief Ugo heard Chidi had come back home, he visited him at his father's house and was so happy for Chidi's arrival. What impressed him the most was that Chidi had returned home alive. However, Chief Ugo was troubled that for all these years, Chidi had been gone without a trace. He was the one who had sent him to town to live with Okoro. He'd been responsible for Chidi, afraid something might have happened to him. When Okoro had reported his escape to Chief Ugo, he'd been unhappy. He'd done all he could to find Chidi's whereabouts, but no one had seen or heard from him until the day Alice received his letter. That was the day Chief Ugo regained his sanity.

Chidi took him to see his new car. He hadn't forgotten the help Chief Ugo rendered to ensure that his secondary education was completed; nor had he missed the effort the chief had made to alleviate his suffering after his father's death.

Chief Ugo left his house that day, but Chidi later visited him with some gifts. It was during this visit that Chidi told him about his life with Okoro and what had made him run away with the clothes he had taken to sell. He assured him that he would pay Okoro back.

Later, Chidi went to Okoro's house to pay him back, but Okoro refused to accept the money. He told Chidi he had forgiven him and apologized for mistreating him. On that day, Chidi and Okoro reconciled.

The most interesting thing Chidi told Chief Ugo was that he planned to rebuild his father's house. He asked him to help him find people who would rebuild the house. Chief Ugo agreed.

He was very impressed with Chidi's plan. He encouraged him and congratulated him for having such foresight. The idea of rebuilding his father's house made Chief Ugo believe Chidi had the same knowledge as his father. He had precisely followed the same wisdom his father had when he was alive. He strongly believed Chidi would do more than his father in Umueze. He encouraged him to follow in his father's footsteps. Before Chidi left his house, he told Chief Ugo when the building would start.

Chidi wanted to go back to town the following day. Before he left, he gave Alice some money to put Ogechi in school. He was able to resolve some of the problems the family had. Other major problems such as rebuilding the house were resolved through Chief Ugo after he had returned to town.

Chidi took Ogechi's schooling very seriously, just like his father had; he had a lot of love for education. He would have gone to college, but his father's death had robbed him of the opportunity.

Chapter 14

A NEW FRIEND

Mr. Williams completed his duty; after spending five years in Africa, it was time for him to return to America. Another person would be coming from America to replace him. A week before his departure, Chidi and other employees secretly organized a send-off party for him. The employees and other guests were invited. It was a very lively occasion. Food and drinks were abundant. Everyone enjoyed the party.

It was during the party that Chidi met a man named Audo Taiwo, a prominent member of the community. Chidi and Mr. Taiwo introduced each other. They talked about their lives, jobs, and many other things. Mr. Taiwo had worked as a civil servant for twenty-five years, and he had currently retired. He was a very dedicated and hardworking man. A man of integrity, his attitude toward work helped him to progress rapidly in his job. He loved to associate with different people, regardless of their status and ages.

He didn't like dishonest people. He liked to associate himself with people of integrity and would disassociate himself from those who didn't have integrity once he knew the person better.

Mr. Taiwo had a cousin he'd never liked because of his dishonesty. This person could never be trusted with anything that involves money. Mr. Taiwo had learned this the hard way after he trusted his cousin with a large sum of money. That was when Audo had been a student abroad. Before his graduation from the university, Mr. Taiwo planned to make life better for himself. While he was in school, he worked at night to save some money he would use to build a house in his village. For six years, he lived abroad; Mr. Taiwo saved about fifteen thousand pounds. That was the money he sent to his cousin to build a house for him while he was still abroad, studying. His cousin Joe gave him the assurance that before he returned to the village, the house would be completed.

To Mr. Taiwo's surprise, after he finished his education and went back to the village to move into his new house, there weren't any bricks put together for the house. Cousin Joe had taken the money and built his own house instead. It took the kinsmen of the village quite some time to settle the matter before Audo could take back the ownership of his house. That was how Audo Taiwo learned the hard way. That experience had taught him a great lesson not to trust anybody with money, and he had decided not to befriend dishonest people.

During his conversation with Chidi, Mr. Taiwo discovered that Chidi must be a good man. He'd heard about Chidi when he was living with the white man in the city. He began to like him. He saw him as somebody he could relate to. They both enjoyed talking to each other. Before the party was over, both exchanged telephone numbers so they could keep in touch in the future.

On the day Mr. Williams left for America, Chidi drove him to the airport. Mr. Williams gave him some information he would need to keep in touch with him after he'd returned to America.

Back in the office, Chidi was temporarily taking care of two positions in the company: his own managerial position and the supervisory position Jack Williams had left behind. The company's workload didn't suffer much after Mr. Williams left. Chidi often worked late to keep the business moving forward until Mr. Williams's replacement arrived.

During this busy time, Chidi couldn't visit his village though he had planned to start rebuilding his father's house. He had to send a message to Chief Ugo with some money to start buying building materials for the house. Chief Ugo hired a contractor to demolish the old house and start building the new one. Before the old house was torn down, Chidi made an arrangement with Chief Ugo for Alice and her daughter to move with his family until the new house was completed. The people in the village were very excited when they saw Chidi was about to build a new house in their village.

The rebuilding of Chief Udo's house by his son was evidence that Chidi had become a successful man. That new house alone had made some people in the village start to make friends with Chief Ugo and his family so that through him they might get to know Chidi. Chidi had never had the chance to visit home again because of his busy work at the factory. The building of the house was still going on. Chief Ugo was doing excellent work.

The house changed. It was no longer the mud house it used to be. It was now a newly constructed house with a corrugated iron roof, the kind usually seen in the township. Light fittings were also installed in the house. Chidi had bought a new generator that would supply lights to the house so anytime he came home, light would be in the house just like the house where he lived in the city. There was no house throughout the village that could compare to the house Chidi was building.

Another new thing Chidi had brought to his house was water borehole that supplies water to the village. Water borehole is a pipe drilled underground with a pumping machine that extract water underneath to the surface thank that stores the water to be used. It was from the surface tank that the drinking water was supplied to Chid's house where the Umueze villagers were allowed to come and fetch their drinking water. That means, they did not have to travel the long distance to fetch water from the stream as they usually do. Chidi made it easy for the villagers to get water from his compound and ease their suffering. The Umueze villagers were pleased about the change of life he had brought to the village. Chief Ugo was the only one in charge of the construction until the work was completed.

Chidi finally came home after several months, when he took leave from his work. He was impressed when he saw the amount of work done in the house. When people noticed Chidi had come back to the village, they began to troop in to see him. Everyone was coming to visit him, including the ladies. Some wanted to make friends with him, while others had come to get something from him.

Due to the number of people coming to see him each day, he decided to shorten his visit. Chidi wasn't ready to befriend any of the women in his village because he didn't know them well. He couldn't relate to them because some of them weren't enlightened. He couldn't see himself developing relationships with the village ladies. He believed those women who came to his house had come to obtain some money he had acquired; it wasn't that they loved him so much.

Before he left, Chidi remembered that Mr. Taiwo had told him he could visit him whenever he traveled across his area. Since Chidi was close to Mr. Taiwo's town, he decided to visit him. He telephoned him to get directions to his house. Later, Chidi arrived at his house and rang the doorbell.

A young boy, Mr. Taiwo's youngest son, answered the door. Chidi wanted to make sure he was at the right house, so he asked, "Is this Mr. Taiwo's house?"

"Yes," the boy answered. "He has just gone to see a friend in the next building, but my mother is here." The boy told the visitor to wait at the door so he could let his mother know about Chidi's presence. He went back inside and told his mother a man was at the door, looking for his father.

"Do you know him?" the mother asked.

"No," the boy replied, "but he said he was looking for my father, and—"

"Let me go and see the man. Where is he?"

"He is waiting outside," the boy answered.

The mother went to the door and saw him.

"Good day, madam," Chidi said. "I'm looking for Mr. Taiwo. Am I in the right place?"

"Yes, you are in the right place," the woman answered. "Are you Mr. Chidi Udo from Umueze village?"

"Yes, madam."

"My husband told me about your visit." She ushered him inside to the living room. She told Chidi that her husband has just gone out to see their neighbor and would be right back.

Mrs. Taiwo welcomed him and advised him to wait for her husband to return.

Chidi waited patiently. She went into the kitchen to get Chidi something to drink. Chidi gazed around the living room. He saw a couple of pictures on the wall. Among them were wedding and family pictures. Those pictures added a lot of beauty to the living room. There were many other decorations in the room, including a large ceramic duck with flowers in it.

As Chidi looked at the family pictures on the wall, he noticed Mr. Taiwo had two boys and three girls. The first son lived in London, where he was attending school. The youngest was the one he'd met at the door. The three girls usually lived with their parents, but they were currently living at school.

Among the children, Chidi saw a young, beautiful black girl in one of the family pictures. While he gazed at the picture on the wall, Mrs. Taiwo came into the room with some refreshments. She gave him some drinks and garden eggs in a saucer. "I hope you will like it," she said.

"Yes," Chidi replied with thanks.

While he was enjoying his drinks, the young girl

in the picture caught his attention once again, and he wanted to know more about her. He wanted to ask Mrs. Taiwo about the girl, but he thought it would be inappropriate to do so. As he was contemplating that, suddenly there was a knock on the door.

Mrs. Taiwo went to the door. It was her husband. "Hello, darling. Chidi is waiting for you in the living room."

"That's why I was hurrying home to meet him. I knew he must have been waiting for quite some time. How long has he been here?"

"About thirty minutes," his wife answered.

"I'm sorry for keeping him waiting," he said.

Mrs. Taiwo took two bottles of beverages from her husband and went straight into the kitchen. Mr. Taiwo walked directly to the living room to meet his friend. As he walked toward the room, he cheerfully called Chidi's name in a loud voice.

"Mr. Udo, the executive manager!" he exclaimed. Almost at the same time, he walked into the living room. Chidi responded immediately after he heard his name.

"I'm sorry for keeping you waiting," Mr. Taiwo apologized.

"Don't worry," Chidi advised.

"Have you had anything to eat?" Mr. Taiwo asked.

"Of course. I just finished the second round of

refreshments," Chidi replied. "Your wife is an excellent woman. She has already offered me something to eat."

"Oh, thank you for your compliment," Mrs. Taiwo responded.

Mr. Taiwo called his wife, margi. That was his usual way of calling her, instead of calling her full name, Margaret. She answered from the other room and came to see Mr. Taiwo.

"Please bring the wine from the fridge and get lunch ready," he requested.

A few minutes later, Margi brought the wine and two glasses of wine and returned to the kitchen to prepare lunch. While they were drinking, they talked about Mr. Williams's send-off party, hosted by Chidi. While they were chatting, Chidi turned to Mr. Taiwo and asked, "Are those people in the picture your children?"

"Yes, they are all my children," Mr. Taiwo answered.

"Who is the young lady in the middle, the one standing beside you?"

"Oh, that's my youngest daughter, Laura. She is a student at the government college in Rusby," he replied.

Chidi memorized her name as soon as Mr. Taiwo mentioned it. Although Mr. Taiwo later told Chidi the names of his other children, he could remember only Laura's name. That was the one he liked.

After a few minutes, the little boy came to his

father and told him the food was on the dining table. Mr. Taiwo and Chidi went to the table to have lunch. The dining table was covered with a nice, colorful tablecloth.

"Serve yourself," Mr. Taiwo said to Chidi as they sat down to eat. Chidi was a little shy and ate very sparingly; Mr. Taiwo and his wife busily filled their plates. The food was delicious. Chidi had eaten good food before, but he'd never tasted food like Mrs. Taiwo's.

Chidi was very impressed with the cordial reception Mr. Taiwo and the wife had given him. He enjoyed their hospitality and was certainly glad to begin a new friendship with Mr. Taiwo and his family.

Chapter 15

MR. TAIWO'S VISIT

It had been a while Chidi visited his friend, Mr. Taiwo. He was still very busy with the office work at the clothes factory. No one had filled the position Mr. Williams left vacant, and Chidi was still working both jobs.

Mr. Taiwo knew he hadn't seen his friend for quite some time. They had talked to each other only over the phone. Mr. Taiwo was also busy with his own work. After he retired from the government work, he opened a super store, where he sold all kinds of provisions. He'd been managing the business since his retirement.

Mr. Taiwo unexpectedly visited Chidi when Mr. Taiwo went to town to collect some money due from a customer who had bought some items from his store. He used the opportunity to visit Chidi, his friend. He came with his daughter, who was spending her holidays at home. They were to return home after visiting his friend. Mr. Taiwo knew about the clothes factory, but he hadn't been there since Chidi started working there. Chidi had told him about his place of work the first time they'd met at the send-off party. Mr. Taiwo later found his way to the factory.

He knocked at the door and walked into the reception area with his daughter. Chidi was busy when they came to his office. He was compiling a list of new applicants who had applied for employment at the company. A lot of work was waiting for him at the production line as well. The work had to be completed before he could begin to interview the new applicants; the interview date for the new applicants was to start in about two weeks. Chidi had received a message from his boss to take over his former position and to employ another person locally to take over his supervisory position. This would help to give him some relief.

Almost two years had passed since Mr. Williams went back to America; he couldn't find anybody willing to live in Africa and do the job Chidi was doing. So Chidi was the next choice they had at the moment. Chidi was getting ready to hire somebody who would take over the supervisory job.

The office was separated into two sections. The entrance to the office had a reception area, which led to the main office. Mr. Taiwo and his daughter were waiting at the front desk when the receptionist went to inform her boss about his visitors. A few minutes later, they were called inside.

The main reason Mr. Taiwo went to visit Chidi was to invite him for a welcome-home party he was getting ready to host for his older son, who was studying overseas. He had just finished his university education and was about to come home.

"Come in," Chidi said after he heard the knock on the door. Mr. Taiwo and his daughter appeared, and everyone greeted each other. Chidi immediately recognized the woman.

"You must be Laura," Chidi said.

As she was about to answer, the father interceded with, "That was the young lady you saw in the picture. She came back a few weeks ago on school break. All the children have come back from school." He paused and proceeded to the main issue. We plan to celebrate his graduation from the university. I came to invite you to the event."

After discussing some other issues with Chidi, he got up to leave.

"Do you want to leave now? Please, why not wait for some snacks and beverages?" Chidi insisted.

"No, no, we are not ready to eat anything at this moment," Mr. Taiwo explained.

"Don't say no for your daughter. If you can't, perhaps your daughter may like to have something to drink or perhaps some snacks." Chidi opened his drawer and brought out some snacks for Laura to choose from. She took one and thanked him.

"Okay, I will certainly be present at the party," Chidi said. "Thank you, Mr. Taiwo, for stopping by."

"Thank you too, Mr. Udo, for having us," Mr. Taiwo replied.

"Goodbye, Mr. Taiwo, and to you, too, Laura." They departed.

After they drove away, Chidi thought fondly of Laura. The snacks he had brought out for Laura to take were intended to asses her behavior and see whether she was greedy. Laura hadn't taken more than one snack from him, and she'd been very thankful. That response meant she wasn't greedy. Chidi liked what he had seen in her. He realized Laura was more beautiful in real life than in the picture. He believed her beauty must have increased.

"She is really beautiful," he soliloquized and nodded in amazement.

As Chidi was assessing her in his mind, Laura was caught in the same mood. On their way home, she asked her father, "Who is this man we just visited?"

"He is a friend of mine. His name is Chidi. I met him at a send-off party he organized for his boss two years ago. He is now in charge of the company we just visited."

"I wondered how he knew my name."

"He visited our house while you were in school. He saw your picture, and I told him your name."

"He must be a good man," she asserted.

"Why? What have you seen in him that makes him a good man?" her father asked with a strong voice to end the conversation.

"I mean, his attitude shows he is kind." The discussion ended a few yards away from their house.

Chapter 16

THE HOME PARTY

It was a pleasant occasion. The music vibrated loudly from the two speakers standing in the corner. A third one had been placed inside the living room, and the fourth was at the door leading outside.

Mrs. Taiwo was busy in the kitchen, preparing food for the party. She didn't need much help, so only a few of her friends were contributing to that.

The guests started to come; among them was their noble friend Chidi. Later, the party began in full swing. There was an open dance for everybody, and Mr. Taiwo's children were there. Laura, who had been at school for quite some time, had a lot of dancing experience. She displayed her talents very well. Chidi used the opportunity to get to know Laura before the party ended.

It rained very heavily that day. Those who couldn't leave before the rain started had to wait for it to stop. Chidi waited too. He used the opportunity to have an in-depth conversation with Laura. During this time they had the chance to exchange information with each other.

Chidi went home after the rain subsided. He was happy he'd had the chance to develop some good relationship with Laura.

After the holiday was over, Mr. Taiwo's children went back to their various schools. Audo junior back overseas to begin his master's degree program. As Chidi developed his affection for Laura, she did the same for Chidi. She wrote to him and invited him to visit her at school. He replied, giving her a definite date when he would come.

Laura wanted to have more opportunities to be with Chidi. She would have cherished the time so much if Chidi would pay her a visit soon. Though they hadn't known each other long, she was eager to learn more about him.

On the appointed day, Chidi dressed up and went to see Laura. His school was about forty kilometers from town. He had to leave early to save time.

On the outskirts of town, the road leading to the school was very wide and well paved; since he was driving, he entered a narrower way. Some parts of the road had eroded. It wasn't a smooth journey as he had thought it would be.

As he drove along, the weather started to change. The sky became cloudy, and it began to rain. The road became worse. The rain started to splash heavily on his windshield.

Chidi turned on the wipers and reduced his speed. The road was slippery, and he tried as much as he could to control his steering until the rain let up.

Before the rain ended, he was already at the school. He saw some students trooping in and out from the school premises.

The school was busy and crowded, as if it were a marketplace. He stopped his car and asked some students passing by whether they could direct him to the female dormitory where he could find Laura. When he went down from his vehicle to enter the school, luckily Chidi met a young lady who was a friend of Laura's. She took him to her hostel.

When Laura saw Chidi, she was extremely happy. She ran to him and hugged him. "Oh, Chidi, darling, I have been waiting so long to see you. What was keeping you?" she cheerfully asked.

Chidi was also happy to see her. Before he arrived, Laura had waited with great anticipation. She'd left her hostel and stood at the entrance of the school, waiting. She wondered what could have delayed him. She had earlier watched each vehicle's license plate that passed by, hoping to see Chidi's car. After waiting so long and not seeing his car, she went back to her dormitory. She had just returned to her room for a few minutes when somebody brought Chidi to her hostel.

Her room wasn't conducive to hosting her guest because of the other students living in the same room with her. Laura took Chidi with her to the school hall, where they had the chance to be with each other privately. They discussed all they could that day. If it had been possible, Laura wouldn't have allowed him to go. She had spent almost five hours with him. The evening was fast approaching; the sun was about to set. Chidi looked at his watch. It was almost five o'clock.

"Darling," he exclaimed with surprise, "it's getting late. I have to go."

She reluctantly turned to him and said, "Why not stay until five?"

"I know you want me to stay with you for some more, but please let me go. It is getting later. Tomorrow is another day," he pleaded.

She grudgingly saw him off. On his way home, Chidi wanted to stop and see his old classmate Zach Bello before he returned home. But it was getting late, so he changed his mind and went home.

Laura went back to her hostel. After Chidi's departure, she became lonely and began to worry about him. She was sad because it would take quite some time for her to see him again. She had to do something not to think about him for now. She went to her room to get her books ready to study for her exams. She went to the library; at least she could forget Chidi for the time being.

Laura was very serious about her studies because the examination schedule was already out. If it was possible, she could have spent all her time in the library studying because she didn't want to fail any of her classes. The conditions of their examinations were too strict. If anyone was caught cheating, expulsion was the penalty. All the students were careful to avoid being accused of cheating.

Laura was a bright student like Chidi. She received good grades and was very sure of passing all her exams.

Chapter 17

THE ILLICIT AFFAIR

The house Chidi had started to build two years ago was finally completed. He gave Alice and her daughter a two-bedroom flat. The house was the only one of its kind in the village, and it gained the admiration of the villagers. They also enjoyed the water he provided for them.

Chidi also erected a monument of his father with an epitaph commemorating his death. It was built in front of the house.

Chidi could recall the day he'd visited Laura at school and the reluctance she'd felt when he was about to leave. She had seriously fallen in love with him to such an extent that she never ceased to talk about him.

As their relationship became more serious, Chidi decided to let Laura know he would like to spend the rest of his life with her. She had accepted his marriage proposal, but he hadn't made his plan to marry Alice known to her parents. Inside Chidi's office drawer were several friendship cards Laura had sent him. Chidi had also sent a couple of cards to Laura, all in the name of love. They had so much trust in each other. Chidi didn't believe Laura would succumb to another man.

Laura was always a hard-working student. She was very brilliant and never failed any of her examinations. But she had a big challenge in her academics, which had delayed her studies.

Laura regularly attended the class of a professor who had his eye on her. One day he approached Laura, wanting her to be his girlfriend. But Laura refused. On several occasions, he tried to have an affair with her, but she refused. He tried so many things to get to her but failed.

Then the teacher decided to make Laura fail the course unless she complied with his demands. This was a very challenging moment for Laura, and it would bring some setbacks in her school career. If she said no, she couldn't graduate with other students when she should have graduated. She would have to repeat one or two semesters for the same course. She couldn't report the problem to the school authorities because she was afraid of what the teacher might do to her. Repeating the class over would cost more of her money and time.

After she couldn't go through the problem anymore, she decided to sleep with him because somebody had told her that some students slept with their professors before they could pass their classes.

The immoral affair, the dream of the lecturer, came true. A few weeks after she slept with the professor, Laura didn't see her period again. She began to monitor her body.

Weeks turned to months, and still Laura didn't see her menstrual period. She was worried and disturbed. She knew the pregnancy was due to the affair she'd had with the professor.

Laura was so embarrassed. She thought about what she should do. She worried about her boyfriend, Chidi. What would be his reaction when he discovered she was pregnant by another man? She knew Chidi wouldn't take it lightly, and he would probably end their relationship. Laura was so afraid. She didn't know what the future held for her with Chidi. She was seriously in trouble.

She had to go back to her teacher and talk to him about the problem and any possible solution. The man knew he was responsible for her pregnancy, but he denied it. He advised her to remove the pregnancy.

Laura didn't want to put her relationship with Chidi in jeopardy. She had to do something before the condition became worse. The next thing to do was to take the teacher's advice and terminate the pregnancy.

The teacher paid the medical expenses in full. He referred her to a medical expert, named Dr. Bello, who specialized in removing unwanted pregnancies. Dr. Bello had obtained his medical degree from one of the prestigious universities in Europe on an academic scholarship.

After she left the teacher's office, she went straight to see the doctor. After consulting with the doctor, she was scheduled to return in two days.

Laura returned to her dormitory, knowing her trouble would be over in two days. In the hostel, she was afraid, not knowing the outcome of her procedure. When other students were leaving for their evening studies, Laura didn't go with them. She told them she wasn't feeling well; maybe she was suffering from malaria, she said. Since malaria is a common illness in Africa, people tend to attribute it to every illness, even when it's not. In Laura's case, she knew it wasn't. She told them she would make arrangement to see her doctor soon. They left her and went to their evening studies. But her friend Lucy didn't join the other students that night; rather, she stayed with Laura that night so she wouldn't feel too bad.

In two days, she went to the hospital alone, though Lucy offered to go with her. She didn't want anybody to accompany her to the hospital. She wanted to keep her pregnancy a secret. At the hospital, she was treated with some drugs and advised to purchase additional medicine from the drugstore. She bought the medicine and took it according to the doctor's prescription. The professor paid all the medical expenses in full.

After few weeks later, Laura regained her normal health and saw her period again. She was very happy the trouble was over without Chidi knowing about it. She began her normal life and resumed her studies. After the affair with the teacher, she was allowed to pass the course and move on with other class work. She resumed her life again with her friends at school.

The same week Laura regained her health, Chidi made a surprise visit to see her without knowing what had happened to her. He was on a business trip to a nearby town and decided to stop by to see her. Both were glad to see each other again. They stayed together and chatted over a number of issues all day long.

Laura told him about her recent ill health but didn't elaborate on the sickness. It was on this visit that Chidi proposed to marry her. Laura accepted his offer with joy. She was happy about the proposal, and moreover, she was more delighted that her fiancé didn't know about what had happened to her in school. She did what she could to keep the affair secret. She knew quite well that if Chidi had known about the affair, the proposal wouldn't have taken place. The next thing Chidi wanted to do was to tell Laura's parents his plan to marry their daughter.

After visiting Laura, Chidi drove by to see his old classmate Zach Bello in his clinic, which he hadn't been able to do during his last visit. At the time of his visit, he didn't come with his own vehicle. The car was left in the shop, where it was being repaired. The chauffeur who brought him on this trip took him to Henry Avenue, were Dr. Bello's clinic was located.

Chidi recently discovered that his former classmate at Umueze High School had opened a medical clinic after he returned from abroad. He was pleased for his friend's great achievement and wanted to pay him a visit. When he arrived, he entered the clinic and asked for the doctor; the nurse at the reception desk went to inform Zach Bello that someone by the name of Chidi Udo was looking for him. When she mentioned his name, Dr. Bello immediately remembered him. Chidi had to wait a moment for the doctor to finish with his patient.

The hospital looked very much like a residential home. Someone could easily mistake the clinic for a family home. It was the name outside the clinic that would make someone believe the place was a clinic.

Chidi was sitting in the reception room, where patients normally waited for the doctor to see them, when he suddenly heard someone screaming from the next room.

It was a patient who was being treated. She had just received an injection and couldn't endure the pain, so she cried out. Chidi remembered his childhood home at the Nursey; there he had been given an injection when he was sick. He'd cried so hard that day until a woman came by and gave him some candy. A few minutes later, a bell rang inside the room, and then the nurse told Chidi to come inside to see the doctor.

As soon as Chidi walked inside the room, he saw Zach Bello, and they greeted each other.

"Hello, Dr. Bello."

"Ah, welcome, Chidi." They greeted each other simultaneously. "Is it Chidi Udo?"

"Yes, that's me."

"It's being a long time," Dr. Bello said.

"Yes indeed."

"How did you find me?" Dr. Bello asked.

"Our former student Okezie Ibe told me about you."

"Yes, he came to the clinic for treatment a couple of weeks ago after he learned about it," Dr. Bello explained.

"Okezie Ibe, the great football player," Chidi added.

Mr. Ibe had reminded them of the school days when the schools in the districts usually played in their interschool football competition. Mr. Ibe had been the football captain at Umueze High School and led the school to the finals. Unfortunately, the school had lost the finals at the penalty shootout. Though the school had lost that season, Okezie had come back the next season and redeemed the school. He was remembered for his brilliant performance during the final match between Umueze Secondary School and

Umuola High School. Both teams played tirelessly for ninety minutes without scoring a goal. The referee awarded an extra fifteen minutes; it was then that Okezie surprisingly scored the winning goal. It was the happiest moment for the school. Since he was the captain of the team, the golden cup was handed over to Okezie on the field. At that moment, the celebration started. Students danced across the village to the neighboring village in celebration of their victory in that season. Okezie's and the school players' photo still hung in the sports office in Umueze Secondary School for remembrance.

After greeting each other, the doctor showed him to a seat. They started chatting, jumping from one subject to another, not finishing the last. They talked about so many issues, ranging from their secondary school days to their present social commitments. It was then that the doctor told him the sad story of a young girl who had recently visited his clinic. How beautiful she'd been. The problem was that the young lady was one of those girls who slept around. She had come to receive female treatment.

Dr. Bello was somebody who lust after women, especially the beautiful ones. The doctor liked her looks, but couldn't trust such a layabout. Chidi asked who she was, and he told him the woman's name and where she had come from. Immediately, Chidi knew it was Laura. He was puzzled and tried to hide his feelings, pretending he didn't know the lady the doctor was talking about. Chidi was disappointed in her.

Dr. Bello used to have a lot of female friends in those days in school. He came from a rich family and always had money to spend on girls. Though he messed around with girls, he never played with his education. He was a bright student, always on top of his class; that was the reason his parents cared much about him. When he was in school with Chidi, everyone knew Zach was going to be successful because of his intelligence. Zach Bello's parents lived in the city. When he was in the city school, he was too much into girls. His parents were afraid something wrong may happened to him if they didn't do something about his flirtation with girls. They took him from the city to live with his uncle in the village and attend village school to avoid the distractions from his female friends in town.

After chatting with his friend, Chidi left his office. He was sad about the information from the doctor concerning Laura. He wondered whether Laura could be deceiving him. The news was a big burden to Chidi that night.

For Laura, the cat had been let out of the bag, but she didn't know this.

The semester was coming to an end with pending examination ahead. Laura was serious about her studies as always. She completed her exams and packed all her belongings for the semester break. Laura, who hadn't seen her fiancé for quite some time, visited him. That was when Chidi poured his heart out to her concerning her misdeed. He couldn't believe what Laura, his jewel of great value, had done.

Chidi insisted on knowing why she had involved herself in that ugly act. Tears began to stream down her cheeks as Chidi insisted on finding out the truth from her.

"I didn't mean to hurt your feelings. It was a trial that came upon me, which I couldn't overcome. Please forgive me," she cried, and she explained what had happened to her.

After hearing her story, Chidi realized Laura had acted in frustration. Now he knew she cheated on him out of frustration to pass her exams.

Chidi planned to confront the teacher, but later he changed his mind because going after the teacher would have brought more embarrassment to his fiancée and himself. Having an abortion was a sensitive topic, and he didn't want to make the matter public. He wanted to avoid becoming a laughingstock. They both kept the matter to themselves. He remembered how close he was to Laura's father; he didn't want the problem to escalate.

Chidi told Laura he had let go of the affair because of her father, who had been a good friend. He believed

Laura should have done something else other than sleeping with the teacher to pass the class.

Also, he didn't want to have misunderstandings with the family since he planned to marry their daughter. Laura pleaded with him to forgive her, and Chidi accepted her plea and decided to let peace reign.

Chapter 18

CHIDI MARRIES LAURA

The immense love Chidi had for Laura was the actual reason for making peace with her. Meanwhile, Chidi went to Mr. Taiwo to inform him of his decision to marry his daughter. Mr. Taiwo didn't refuse; he knew Chidi was a man of unquestionable character.

After they discussed the marriage, Mr. Taiwo met with his daughter to hear from her whether she had accepted Chidi's proposal to marry her. Laura and Chidi had been friends for over two years, but her father wasn't aware of that. All he knew about Chidi was that he was a good friend who talked to everyone in his family. Mr. Taiwo knew marriage should be a decision between the two people involved and not depend on a third party. He believed the time had gone when parents should decide whom their children should marry. In that way nobody would be held accountable for anything that came out of the relationship. The marriage was now a matter between Laura and Chidi.

After Chidi made their engagement known to her family, he told Chief Ugo and Alice, who would play the part of his parents in the marriage. According to the custom and tradition of Umueze, the wedding usually took place at night, but Chidi didn't want to get married at night. He wanted to get married during the daytime as it was done in the city. He had already decided to have his wedding done in the city. The custom of Umueze also allowed male children to wed only after they have been initiated or admitted in the village cultural society.

Chidi hadn't reached the age of initiation when his father died. He hadn't been initiated as his father had earlier promised him before his death. As a result, he wouldn't be permitted to have his marriage done in his village unless he performed what the custom required of him.

Chief Ugo wanted to initiate him into the cultural society when he visited home, but Chidi refused to be initiated. He had already made up his mind not to have his wedding in his village. Also, after spending most of his life in the city, he was leaning more toward a Christian life than toward his village culture. He believed it would be a good idea to have the wedding done in the city, where he knew most people. Chidi barely knew anybody in the village, except his stepmother, his sister, and Chief Ugo.

To initiate the actual marriage, Chidi had to prepare to pay Laura's bride-price to her parents before they could marry. Chidi had to wait another year when Laura would graduate from college to bring the money to her parents.

While she was finishing school, Chidi got the pride-price ready for his in-laws.

When graduation day came, Laura did well in all her classes. She finished with the upper class. During the graduation event, Audo Taiwo, Margaret, their children, and Chidi were there at the school to support her. When the time came, the graduating students lined up and matched into the school auditorium. Each department wore garments that distinguished them from each other. After the graduating students and guests were seated, there was an opening payer, followed by a welcome address from the dean of the college faculty.

Then the handing over of the degrees began; each student went forward to receive his or her degree as his or her name was called. People cheered their students as their names and degrees were called out. After a couple of students were called out, Laura Taiwo was called to get her degree. As soon as her name was announced, Chidi and her family screamed, "Go, Laura. You are the best. Congratulations." She waved, moved forward, and reached out for the diploma. Immediately, Chidi took her picture.

After the degree presentation was over, students moved from the hall in a single file until everyone left the auditorium. Friends, families, and well-wishers went outside and began taking photos with the graduates. At the end of the day, the event was over. Everyone left the school and went home. Mr. Taiwo took Laura and his family, together with Chidi, to a restaurant to entertain and celebrate her academic success. Everybody ate and drank to celebrate her graduation. Laura was happy that school was over; she was ready for the next stage of her life.

A month after Laura graduated, Chidi told his in-laws the day he would come to pay Laura's bride-price. On that day Chidi took three of his employees to go with him to meet his in-laws. One of them was an elderly man from the village of Ikpeama, who worked in the factory with him; his name was Zebulon Amoji. Chidi had asked him to go with him because Mr. Amoji knew the village tradition well. Chidi also sent for Chief Ugo and Alice to meet them at Mr. Taiwo's village at Ikpeama. Zebulon Amoji and Audo Taiwo came from the same village. Chidi had learned that the last time Mr. Taiwo visited Chidi in his office.

On the day of the event, Chidi and his guest arrived at Mr. Taiwo's house in the village. He came with palm wine and seven shillings, as the tradition allowed. Laura went to the village with her family, too, but she wasn't involved with the bride-price. It was a transaction between Mr. Taiwo's family and Chidi's family. After everybody was seated, Chief Ugo stood up and addressed the families.

"My name is Chief Ugo. I'm a friend of the late Chief Udo, the father of Chidi Udo. On behalf of Chidi Udo, we have come to pay the bride-price for our future wife, Miss Laura Taiwo," Chief Ugo explained.

He brought out a cage of palm wine and the seven shillings, which he presented to Audo Taiwo and other family members. The money was counted to ensure the tradition was fulfilled. Taiwo's family accepted the money, which meant her family had accepted Chidi's request to marry Laura. Taiwo's family brought food, meats, and drinks to the suitor's family to entertain them. Both families ate and drank on that day at Mr. Taiwo's house. After the marriage tradition was fulfilled, Chidi and his guests departed to get ready for the wedding day.

The reason Chidi had decided to have his wedding in the city was to attract more people to the event. He was better known in the city than in his village. After Chidi went back to town, he began to plan for his wedding. In African tradition, when a man is ready to marry, it's his duty to purchase the wedding clothes for himself and his wife. Chidi purchased his suit and sent money to Laura for her wedding dress.

With Margaret's help, Laura bought a nice wedding gown. Before the preparation began, Chidi had already scheduled a date for the wedding. The date was communicated to friends and well-wishers through the distribution of the wedding cards.

When Chidi was about to marry Laura, he thought about how to invite his friend, Zach Bello. He remembered what the doctor had told him about Laura. They hadn't talked to each other lately. Now that Chidi was preparing to marry Laura, he had to invite the doctor to the wedding. To clarify the notion Dr. Bello had in mind about Laura, Chidi let him know that the lady who had come to his clinic for the abortion was his fiancée. Chidi explained to his friend what had transpired in her behavior. He did that so his friend would know his fiancée wasn't the kind of woman the doctor had assumed. Rather, she'd been a victim of circumstance. After he explained the situation to Dr. Bello, he told him his plan to marry her and invited him to the wedding. On the wedding day, Dr. Bello came to support his friend.

On that day, Laura dressed in immaculate velvet, which completely covered her legs to the ground. Her face was dazzling, well lit up. She was filled with immeasurable joy. Beside her was Chidi, dressed very attractively in his black suit. Friends and well-wishers from various places came for the wedding. Chidi didn't forget his boss, Mr. Williams, who had been invited as well, but he couldn't come because of business commitments in America.

Mr. Taiwo had arranged for the wedding to take place in his church. He was a deacon in the Synagogue Missionary Church. That was the church where his family had grown up. Every member of the church knew him well.

At the side of the couple were the chief bridesmaid, a friend of Laura, and the best man to Chidi. The best man was a friend from work. At the wedding, the pastor of the church presented the couple before the congregation.

Both exchanged their vows with the wedding ring and were declared husband and wife. After the vows were done, the pastor offered prayers on their behalf and declared the entertainment of the wedding open. It was then that the couple were ushered to the reception. The flower girls threw flowers on the couple as they walked out of the church to the reception. Among them was Ogechi, a half sister to Chidi, and Lucy Madu, Laura's friend from school. She was the wedding's bridesmaid.

At the reception, there was live music, food, and drinks. Many people were there to witness the best wedding in town. Pictures were taken to mark the event. Many friends and relatives took pictures with Laura and Chidi. At this moment of his life, Chidi wished his parents were alive so someone could take pictures of them and his wife. The people in the family photo with the couple were Alice, Ogechi, Chief Ugo, and Taiwo's family.

As part of the wedding tradition during the reception, the event coordinator brought out the couple to cut the wedding cake. Ceremonial judges were selected to watch the cutting of the cake and decide about what they observed as the cake was cut. At the end, the judges declared that the couple had used equal strength in the cutting of the cake, which meant that as they had done in cutting the cake, working together in one accord would help strengthened and build their new relationship.

Immediately the cake was cut, everybody clapped his or her hands to cheer up the couple. The wedding was over at sunset after all of them had enjoyed themselves at the reception. Therefore, Chidi and Laura officially became husband and wife. They were glad they had become one family.

Chapter 19

CHIDI'S LIFE AFTER MARRIAGE

Only a few people from the village went to the wedding. Chief Ugo, Alice, and the daughter went to the city for the wedding. Chidi had arranged their transportation to the city. He wanted them to witness the wedding since they were the only close family he had. After the wedding, Chidi sent them back to the village.

At the time Laura and Chidi were in friendship with each other, he had told her about his deceased parents and the circumstances surrounding his upbringing. Laura knew that the only family her husband had was Alice and her daughter. As stated in the story, there were many reasons Chidi and Laura's wedding was not done in the village. One of them was that her husband didn't have enough people in the village, except Alice and Ogechi, who would assist him to plan for the wedding. The two family members wouldn't have done much to make a successful event.

After the wedding, Laura traveled with Chidi to visit his village. The husband had promised her that he would take her to his village after their wedding so she could see his village and the new house he had built. She was looking forward to visiting her husband village and seeing their new home.

Alice, her daughter, and Chief Ugo welcomed the couple with open arms. Ogechi had recently finished her secondary school when her brother and wife came to the village. She stayed with them in their house to help Laura do some of the domestic work. The two-week leave the company had given Chidi came to an end, so he had to resume his duty. The couple had to travel back to the city with Ogechi so she could help them at home.

During this period, life seemed rosy for the couple. They lacked nothing and were economically fit to solve any financial problem arising in or outside the family. But after three years of good marriage, there was an economic change, and the raw material for the clothes factory was no longer as available as it used to be. The industry gradually began to decline in production. Things were tough. The company began to laid of some of their workers.

The situation greatly affected Chidi. He sent a message to Mr. Williams, the company's founder and director in America. Mr. Williams, after he went back to America, he had been exporting the raw materials used in making the clothes. He could no longer export materials to Africa due to an embargo imposed on the raw materials going to Africa. Some of the newly imported raw materials were confiscated at the sea port, so Mr. Williams could do nothing to improve the company's business condition. The company employees stopped their last production after the raw materials in their warehouse were depleted. The last salary was paid to the few employees retained after the first retrenchment.

Chidi had been making some connections to see whether the situation would change for the better, but it didn't work. He resorted to join his wife in managing their medicine store to avoid being idle. Chidi had opened the medicine store for Laura when she couldn't secure a job in her field. At the moment, she was managing the store by herself. The store was Lucy's idea.

After her marriage, Lucy and Laura's friendship became stronger. Both friends had graduated at the same time from the university. Because Lucy hadn't secured employment after their graduation, she spent most of her time with her friend Laura. During the time she spent more time with Laura, she suggested that her friend convince her husband to open a medicine store for her, since pharmacy had been her major program in school. Laura took her advice and convinced her husband, who later opened the store.

It was during that close association with Laura that she started brainwashing her as well. When Lucy saw Laura's hard work and dedication to her family, she became jealous. She told her friend it wasn't right for her husband to leave the family duty for her to do alone. She even asked Laura whether her mother had ever done what she was doing in her father's house. It was that comment that changed Laura's attitude toward her husband.

There was a time when the family's condition became worse. Fortunately, Laura was employed outside as a pharmacist in a government medical store after she worked for two years in their own pharmacy store. It was her experience that gave her the opportunity to work in the government establishment. The management of their store became the sole responsibility of her husband with the help of Ogechi.

After Laura was employed, her resources began to supplement the money derived from their private business. Their condition changed for the better. Their standard of living began to improve from what it used to be. The happiness that had left their family during this period returned to normal. At that time, Laura conceived to have their first child.

As they were praying for better times, misfortune struck again. This time burglars came and looted some of their belongings. One morning Chidi walked into the living room only to discover that some of their belongings had been stolen. The door leading to their living room from the outside had been broken. Chidi raised an alarm, attracting the attention of his wife, who rushed from their bedroom and saw things for herself. Almost everything in the living room was gone; the room was empty. When Chidi looked at the broken door more closely, he was surprised by the way the thieves had broken into the house without arousing their attention. This was when he began to believe the thieves may have been operating with some mystic.

A lot of things were stolen: all their furniture, a video set, a television set, and a stereo. That morning Chidi reported the stolen items to the police; the police came and took an incident report. A few days later, two suspects were apprehended and detained. After the police couldn't find any connection between the stolen property and those arrested, police later released the suspects and set them free. The investigation continued for quite some time. After they couldn't catch the burglars, the case was closed. Chidi decided to sell off their only vehicle to replace the stolen items, but his wife discouraged him and offered to help replace the stolen properties.

Chapter 20

RECONCILIATION

The family was unhappy about their stolen belongings. The theft of the house goods was a huge economic setback for the family. They started to find a means to replace the stolen items. They used the money Laura had saved for some time to purchase the lost possessions. Chidi was still managing the medicine store. They were still able to make additional income to run their family expenses.

After some months, the couple began to replace some of their stolen property. Laura contributed much to that. From what her friend had taught her, she began to put the bad advice she received from her friend into practice. Laura started to take pride in those things she personally contributed to the house—in fact, to such an extent that she began to disrespect her husband because Chidi couldn't contribute as much as she did.

Chidi started to notice some sudden changes in behavior. Even his sister noticed the same behavior sometimes, based on the way she occasionally talked to him. Chidi couldn't figure out why the sudden change in Laura. She must have thought her husband's values were depreciated after he lost his employment. She elevated herself so high after she noticed Chidi wasn't bringing money to the house like she was. But one funny thing about the recent behavior was that while Chidi had been employed at the clothes factory, she had been a housewife. She'd had no job. He'd provided for all family needs.

Now that the good, old days were gone, the wife had forgotten that he was the same husband who had been taking care of her all those years. Laura must have thought that building a family was a man's sole responsibility, even when the man couldn't afford to do so at a moment in his life. But in an actual sense that wasn't how it works, but her friend had convinced her to believe that. When two people come together as husband and wife, both have a duty to help each other build the family. Anything that affects one must also affect the other. That means each person must take care of the other person, whether good or bad.

Laura had forgotten about the day of their wedding, when the ceremonial judges had watched them cut the cake. The judges had declared that the couple used equal strength in cutting the cake, which meant that just as they had done in the cutting of the cake, working together in one accord would help build their new family. She needed to be reminded of their vows and commitment to one another.

During this time, Laura showed off that she had more education than her husband. Instead of speaking to her husband in their native language, as they were used to, Laura decided to speak big grammar to him just to prove she had more education than he.

Chidi was sad about the recent changes in his own family, which he had molded. He could remember when things had been going well with him, even after he got married. He was a man with a great reputation.

Chidi did his best to handle the problem by himself without disclosing the issue to anybody. He discovered that it was the privilege he had given to Laura to take care of certain things in the house that had made her behavior change. He knew she hadn't behaved this way after their marriage, when she hadn't been financially obligated to help anyway in the house. Now it was Chidi's responsibility to change his house for the better by taking away the privileges he had given to his wife. He had to stop all financial support from Laura.

After he made known to Laura her recent changes of behavior, he also let her know she was no longer allowed to provide any financial help in the house. He would be the sole provider for the house since her support for the house needs had become a problem. Laura wasn't happy with her husband's new decision.

After the new changes in the house, Laura turned her misbehavior against Ogechi in the form of retaliation for Chidi's action. At any moment when her husband wasn't at home, she began to mistreat Ogechi, even to beat her.

When Chidi learned what was happening from her sister, he got his wife's attention and advised her to stop what she was doing to Ogechi, or he would send Ogechi back to the village.

Laura couldn't adhere to her husband's advice. She felt that nobody in the house should tell her what she should or shouldn't do. She continued in her usual way of mistreating Ogechi. When Chidi learned that Laura hadn't listened to his advice, he sent Ogechi back to the village.

When Ogechi finally went back home, she told her mother about what had happened. She also told her mother about the things the burglars had stolen from her brother and about the retrenchment that took place at Chidi's workplace, which had caused her brother to lose his job. Chief Ugo was also told about what had happened to Chidi. He couldn't imagine the things Chidi must be going through at this difficult time. He knew how hard Chidi had suffered in those days when he was a young boy after his father passed away. He had been through a lot to become the man he was today. He had accomplished so much in life that nobody in the village had done. He had completed his new house in the village, erected his father's statue, and built a water borehole for the village.

Like his father, Chidi had been nice to people. He had helped many people in need. He'd built a house for Chief Ugo at the time he built his father's house. He had done that to acknowledge the good work Chief Ugo had done for him after his father died, especially to ensure that Chidi finished his secondary school education. Chief Ugo believed Chidi's setbacks would change for the better because he wasn't the kind of person he wouldn't wish well. Any good thing that came to Chidi went to everybody due to his generosity.

When Alice heard about what had happened to Chidi, she began to pray for him. She knew that when he succeeded, his family and the village people would succeed as well. Alice had thought Ogechi was sent home due to the hard time Chidi was facing. But that wasn't the case; it was Laura's attitude that had sent her back to the village. Chidi didn't want Laura to hurt her or make her life miserable. She was the only sister he had. The family needed her so much.

Ogechi didn't know why she had been sent home. A week before she went to the village, Chidi took her to the market and bought her a lot of things, including a box of clothes. That was when she was told she would be going back to the village to spend some time with her mother and would return to the city after some time. She obeyed her brother and packed her belongings. The next day, Chidi took her to the motor park, where she took transportation back to the village.

A few weeks after Ogechi went back to the village, Laura began to feel her absence. Over the past years when Ogechi was living with them, Ogechi had done most of the work at home. She'd washed their clothes and gone to the market to purchase anything needed at home. After she left, Laura had to do all the work alone at home. The situation became worse now that she had become pregnant. She had to leave home early to get to work and to come back home to finish the work still left undone. While going through the challenges at home, she came to realize the importance of living with Ogechi. As she went through the challenges of doing the work alone at home, Chidi didn't care much about her ordeal. As usual, he would go to the store, do his work, and come back in the evening after his daily work was over.

Laura went through the hardship for quite some time and was tired of the trouble. In addition, her husband refused to come home as usual directly after closing work at the end of the day. Chidi would go somewhere in town to have some drinks with friends and would return home late at night and he would not eat his food. After Laura could no longer put up with the situation, she decided to make peace with her husband.

Chidi came back from the store one evening and was about to drive out to see friends, as he sometimes did. Laura was at home, waiting for Chidi to come back. She heard his vehicle, hoping her husband has returned home to stay. But he walked into the house, dropped his bag, and drove off again. When Laura went to look for him, she realized Chidi had already zoomed off.

"Oh no. So Chidi has gone out again today," she cried. "Now that he has gone, the next time he will be back home will be late at night. Perhaps he will come home drunk and won't pay attention to me, as he did the other night. Okay, I know what to do."

Later, Chidi came back home late and was as drunk as Laura had predicted. She couldn't have a conversation with him that night since he was drunk. She decided to talk to him in the morning.

In the morning, she waited for him to get up from bed. But that day, it took him a little longer; perhaps he was tired from last night. Laura couldn't wait any longer. She went into the bedroom to talk to him. He still lay in bed. She quietly got ahold of him from behind. Chidi stretched himself and turned gradually to see who was behind him, asking, "Who is sneaking behind me?" He knew already who it was. He'd heard the door when Laura came into the room. He was pretending to be asleep.

After he asked the question, which got no answer,

Chidi turned around and saw her without further comment. Laura looked intensely; she was blinking as if something had fallen into her eyes. She expected to hear something from him, but Chidi didn't say anything. Laura's recent attitude reminded him of her past. The mischievous interaction, which she'd had with her professor while she was in school, would have ended their relationship.

The latest change in behavior from Laura would have caused Chidi to end their marriage, but the love he had for her and the baby on the way had changed his intended action.

After gazing at each other momentarily, tears rolled down from her eyes; she hugged him and started to apologize.

"My love, I have caused you anguish, and I can see you are a man of a temperate mind. Your attitude toward me has shown that you really love me.

"I have made you sad and restless in your home, which should have been a resting place for us. But you didn't mind me. Being so tolerant, all you did to express your resentment was to leave early and come back late. I know you chose this way to avoid me. It has been enough; the trouble is over. I have accepted my fault. I know I was responsible for the trouble. I am sorry.

"Misunderstanding is very common in any family, but wise couples like me and you will not allow it to linger. Please, I will not allow it to happen again," she promised.

After listening to her plea, Chidi tried to ignore her but couldn't. Laura then reminded him of the wedding vow they had made at church to love each other forever. She looked at his face and asked him, "Where is the love we promised each other? It looks like the love is fading away; our love is fading away." When Chidi thought about what Laura had just asked him in a gentle voice, he mellowed and forgave her. Laura's plea to her husband made him to understand that she was a wife who could easily admit her faults and to recognize when her husband was offended.

Chidi rose from the bed and hugged his wife as a sign of reconciliation. They gradually rolled back into bed and made up. Laura could hardly recollect the last time she'd had such a romantic moment with her husband since the trouble began. That day their relationship was rekindled.

After they had settled their differences, they began to live their normal lives as husband and wife. They began to find solutions again to their family problems.

It didn't take long after they reconciled their differences that Laura had her baby. As her stomach got bigger before the baby was born, Chidi began to reflect on his own birth, how he'd lost his mother during his birth. That day, as he had been told, his father had gone to the farm to prepare it for the season while his mother was at home, expecting to deliver her child. The father was to return home soon to be with the wife. Unfortunately, the father couldn't make it home on time. The baby started to come out, and eventually the mother delivered the baby, collapsed, and died.

Chidi sometimes thought about his mother's ordeal as his wife's delivery came close. He knew what had happened to his mother wouldn't happen to his wife because the way babies were born nowadays had changed.

During his time, most babies were born at home with no medical help. There was no hospital or clinic as today. Women usually delivered their babies naturally at home; some even had their babies born at the farm, where they had gone to till the land.

It was in the middle of the night when Laura began to feel the baby moving in her belly. Chidi had fallen asleep when his wife woke him and told him the movement of the baby was getting stronger. He jumped up and quickly took the baby's bag, which was already packed. He took Laura to the car and drove her to the hospital.

The couple arrived at the hospital in the middle of the night. Laura was groaning in pain as Chidi walked with her into the maternity ward. They first went to the admission to register her name. At the moment, her pain began to increase. Chidi ran to the head nurse and begged for help. It was the first time he had ever seen a woman in labor. Chidi was so afraid and confused; he didn't know what to do to help his wife.

The head nurse called Laura's doctor, who quickly came in a short period. She was taken straight to the delivery room. Chidi was kept outside the room, where he watched and prayed for the safe delivery of his baby. He could hear from the outside of the room when one of the nurses told her to push. "I say push harder. Your water is broken; the baby is about to come."

Chidi could hear his wife screaming so hard; suddenly, he heard the cry of a baby. That was when he knew he had become a father. A few minutes later, he was called inside the room to see the new baby. "Hold your son. That's a baby boy," the head nurse told him and handed the baby to him.

Chidi cried as he held his baby. Laura was exhausted and happy. Mother and child were doing well. Laura was wheeled out of the delivery room to the maternity ward together with her baby. The nurse told the new mother to feed the baby. Chidi was so excited that morning.

The doctor asked him what he would name his son. He told them he would name him after his father, Prince Udo Chidi. In African custom and traditions, if a man had a son, he would always name the baby after his father. If the baby was a female, the man would name the child after his mother. That was the common way the African people immortalized their parents.

According to tradition, Chidi named his son after his father.

Later, Chidi left Laura and the baby at the hospital and went home to get some rest. He was exhausted after being up all night long without sleep. As soon as he arrived home, he called his in-laws and broke the good news. Since they didn't have a phone in the village, he later sent a message to his stepmother, Ogechi, and Chief Ugo. Everyone was excited about the newborn child.

Laura and the baby had to stay another two days in the hospital before they were discharged. Chidi drove back to the hospital to pick them up. Before the baby came home, Chidi invited his mother in-law to come and stay with them to assist Laura in taking care of the baby. A week after the baby was brought home, Margaret came to live with them. Her presence was a big relief for the couple. She was the one who helped to take care of the baby and other works at home. Ogechi also offered to come for a visit. After a couple of days, she went to visit the baby. She was another help in the house. At this time, she had grown more mature than before. Chidi allowed her to assist more in the store since the mother-in-law was taking more care at home. Both Margie and Ogechi were great help to the family. Due to their presence in the house,

Laura went back to work after spending one month of maternity leave.

After Laura went back to work, Chidi was working at the store and had to devote more of his time to improve it. He had recently made a contact with Mr. William to find out whether they could do something to start a new business venture in Africa, since the embargo on the raw material for the industry hadn't been lifted. It was then that Mr. Williams invited Chidi to visit him in America to see what they could do to bring the business back to life.

The closure of the textile industry in Africa had made the company in America lose some of its revenue, money was no longer transferred to America. Chidi thought it would be a good idea to visit America so they could begin to discuss what they could do to bring the company back to operation. They agreed when Chidi would be visiting Mr. Williams.

The time Chidi planned to travel to America was a few months ahead, but he wanted to spend more time with his new baby and his wife before he traveled. Chidi loved his family, and he wanted to have a large family. At his youthful age, he wanted to have many children, unlike his father, who hadn't been fortunate enough to have many children. Uloma had had only him and then died. Chief Udo later married Alice, who couldn't conceive a child for quite a long period.

She later had only one child late in her life and couldn't have more children.

Chidi had his first child, but after a few months, he was ready to have the second one. Laura was already pregnant for almost nine months. At the end of that week, Laura went to the hospital to deliver her second baby; at this time the baby was a female.

Before she gave birth to the baby, Chidi always made sure Laura went to the hospital for her routine checkup to ensure the baby and mother were healthy. Chidi named the new baby girl after his mother, Uloma. The parents' names he gave to his children went with the African custom and traditions. This was done to transfer the parents' names to the new generation. Chidi had given his parents' names to his two children to immortalize them. Whenever he called the names of his son and daughter, they reminded him of his mother and father. Chidi believed the baby girl resembled his mother, Uloma, while the boy looked like his father, Chief Udo. The children brought back good memories of his parents.

Chapter 21

THE JOURNEY TO AMERICA

While Chidi was taking care of his wife and the new baby, he was also getting ready to travel to America. He knew it was necessary to spend time with his wife and the baby during this period when she was nursing the baby. Since he would soon be traveling and Laura would need somebody at home to help her out with the children while he was gone, he sent for Ogechi to come back to the city and stay with her. The mother who had come to stay with them after the child was born had already gone back home to stay with her husband. All the arrangements for his journey to America were completed. Then he traveled to visit his friend Jack Williams.

Chidi left early that evening for the airport and was one of the first passengers to arrive. It took a couple of hours to board the airplane. As he was waiting, other passengers began to arrive. Before the time of departure, every passenger was instructed to be seated.

"Please fasten your seat belt," said the announcer. Everybody quickly fastened his or her seat belt on both sides. The last announcements were made before the plane started moving down the runway.

At high speed, the plane lifted into the sky with a thundering sound. It was a very long flight. As the plane climbed into the sky, every passenger was told to remain in his or her seat. Chidi felt as if he were thrown down from a high mountain, and he was dizzy. He was afraid, but he took courage. He was able to manage his fear.

Chidi began to have more confidence when he saw a little child run across his seat. That was after the plane had settled in the air. Even though at that time passengers were allowed to use the restroom, Chidi didn't want to get up from his seat. He decided not to drink any liquid to avoid going to the toilet.

If this little boy isn't afraid, why should I be afraid? That thought came to him. He had never traveled by air before. It was his first experience to travel such a long-distance journey. Before the plane took off, the airplane attendant had given the passengers some directions: "Fasten your seat belts; below your seats, there are life jackets in case of emergency. Pull it out from under your seat and use it for your safety."

The flight attendant vividly demonstrated the directions as passengers watched and listened. Some of the frequent travelers already knew the routine and barely paid attention.

All things being equal, and since this was his first time traveling by air, Chidi watched the entire demonstration with curiosity. He realized the possible risk that may involve flying an airplane. That was when he remembered his wife and two children. He imagined being involved in a plane crash and dying. Then he would miss his wife and the two children. He thought about the funny things his children did at home, especially Prince Chidi Udo, his first child. He made his father laugh so much anytime Chidi tried to tell him to say his name.

"What's your name?" Chidi would asked his son.

"My name is Prick," the boy would say instead of Prince. That made his father laugh so hard. Chidi thought about the funny things the children did and said while he was traveling on a plane. Remembering the fun of being around with his family gave him the courage that nothing would happen to him on his journey. The thought that came to his mind was, *Who would care for my family if something happened to me? Could my wife go back to her parents?*

The plane flew several hours in the air. Chidi could easily look through the window. He was surprised when he couldn't see any forest. He remembered the days when he'd taken a train to town; he'd seen many trees speeding as he looked through the window. But this time around there was no vegetation as he looked through the airplane windows. What he could see were some thick clouds like small mountains with different shapes and sizes. It seemed like an endless journey as he continued to look through the window.

A few minutes later, the flight attendants began to move around. Chidi had no idea what they were getting ready to do. It was lunchtime. They began to pass around some food and beverages. Chidi hadn't seen this kind of unique service when he was on the train. Every passenger was served food and beverages, including Chidi. He knew he'd been given nothing while he was on the train. Chidi had thought the reason food and drinks were served on the plane was because of the high cost of the airline and the time and distance it would take passengers to get to their various destinations. Somebody would be hungry and need to be fed. The train he took to the city didn't cost much, and it was a short trip. Passengers usually got off regularly at every station. Every passenger was responsible for his or her own food.

After lunch was served, everybody seemed to be exhausted. Many passengers fell asleep. Chidi couldn't sleep. He didn't feel comfortable with going to sleep on the plane. He could hear some passengers snoring in their deep sleep.

He couldn't believe some people could go to sleep in a fearful place like an airplane. He felt sorry for the flight attendants and pilots, whose job was to frequently travel in an airplane. He believed they were in a high risk. He thought, *If an accident happens, they will all perish with the plane.*

As Chidi pondered all those thoughts, there was an announcement. "Ladies and gentlemen, we are about to land in the next airport to refuel. Please fasten your seat belts."

Gradually, the plane began to descend. Chidi started to feel dizzy again, the same way he'd felt after the plane took off from the airport. The plane later landed. After refueling, the plane took off again for the final flight to America.

As soon as the plane crossed the equator to the United States, Chidi began to observe some climate changes. It was the beginning of the winter season when he arrived in America. There was less wind, but there was some fog all over the atmosphere. It was hard to see through the sky. Some passengers had light winter jackets ready for the season. Chidi had no idea what the weather would be like; he had no winter jacket except the suit he was wearing. It didn't take long, the plane landed. As soon as the plane came down, he started to feel the impact of the change in weather.

Before the plane landed, Jack Williams and his wife were already at the airport, waiting for him. He knew Chidi's plane had landed after checking the plane's information. It would take some time to clear his luggage at customs and immigration. Jack and his wife waited patiently for him until they saw Chidi walking out from the arrival checkout.

As soon as Jack saw Chidi, he called out his name. "Mr. Udo, I'm over here."

Chidi turned and saw him. He didn't recognize Mr. Williams that much. It had been a long time; he saw him at last. In fact, Jack had grown a little older than how he used to look. The same applied to Chidi. He'd been a younger man when Jack left the office and went back to America. Though there were some changes on both friends, they still recognized each other.

As Chidi heard his name, he turned and quickly walked to Jack. They hugged each other. Jack introduced his wife to Chidi, and they greeted each other. They moved across the other side of the aisle to the luggage claim area and waited for his luggage. There were a lot of passengers with many bags on board; because of that fact, they had to wait for his luggage to come out. A few minutes later, his bags arrived, and they were on their way home.

Before Chidi arrived, Jack had reserved a hotel room for him. Jack and his wife drove Chidi straight to his hotel.

While they drove, Chidi initially thought Mr. William and the wife would take him to their house, where he would spend the rest of his visit. He thought this way because in Africa, most visitors stay with their host in the host's home. Whatever food the hosts prepared for themselves was what they would offer to their guest(s). But, unlike the Americans, who would prefer to put their guest in a hotel, where the guest would feel comfortable and have the choice to enjoy what he or she wanted. That was exactly what Jack did for Chidi.

There are two different lifestyles between African people and American people; those lifestyles were based on what they could afford. Because of limited resources in Africa, most people there may not afford to provide that comfortable lifestyle for their guests compared to the lifestyle in America. More Americans can afford to house their guests in more conducive places than Africans can; everything is based on the available resources the person may have. The opportunity for everyone to have resources is available in America but not in Africa.

Jack and his wife brought Chidi to the hotel, where he would be staying during his visit, and drove back home. Jack and his wife treated Chidi well. Mr. Williams frequently called to keep in touch with him. On the second day of his visit, he and his wife took him out for sight-seeing. They took him to an amusement park, where Chidi had the opportunity to get on some of the rides. This was the first time he had been to an amusement park. The ride he liked most was the slow one. He didn't like the fast ones. The first one he rode was a gentle ride. Chidi loved it, and it prompted him to take another ride with Jack. But this one wasn't as gentle as the previous one.

As he got into the ride, he buckled up as he had on the airplane. The ride gently began to climb up in the air. Chidi felt that he could reach the sky. Jack was sitting next to Chidi. Elizabeth was watching from the ground. Jack had asked her to join with them, but she'd refused.

Jack and his wife, Elizabeth, had visited the park previously. Elizabeth didn't like the fast rides. She was scared to death when they first took the ride. She had to watch Jack and Chidi as the ride began to climb up the ridge. At the end of the ridge, the ride began to descend with full speed. Chidi screamed. At the speed and distance the ride was moving, nobody could hear how loud he was screaming. He had never seen anything like that in his life. Chidi prayed for the ride to end so he could get out of the bucket.

Immediately, the ride came to a stop, and Chidi quickly got out. Jack and Elizabeth laughed at him when they remembered the fear on his face during the ride.

After they visited the amusement park, it was time for them to get down to real business. Jack took him to see the company's textile industry. The business was still doing well; they had viable dialogue concerning the troubled business in Africa.

Jack Williams was a Jewish American. His grandfather was one of the first Holocaust survivors who had come to America after they were liberated. The textile business was a family business. It was Jack's grandfather who had started the business when he first arrived in America. After he passed away, William Judah, Jack's father, took over the company. Jack Williams had left his professional career and joined the family business.

Chidi embraced the lifestyle he saw in America. After two weeks, he started to get used to the way things were done there. He would have loved it so much if he had the opportunity to visit more often. He would prefer to remain in America than to go back home, but with his family in Africa, staying in America wouldn't happen. He made Jack aware of the hard time he'd gone through at home.

Jack gave him some money to support him when he went back to Africa and promised to send more money for him monthly as wages. He assured him that the company wouldn't relent in finding a solution to the problem of the company in Africa.

Chidi had to stay a little longer in America, but since he had left his wife and children for quite some time, he decided to finalize his meeting with Jack so he could go home to see his family. While Chidi was in America, he was still communicating with his wife, Laura. He spoke with her almost every week to know how his children were doing.

Whatever must have happened, Chidi didn't call home the previous week. The following week, when he called home, trouble struck. He was told that his house had caught on fire, but nobody was hurt. When he received the message, Chidi hastened his journey home. After he told Jack about the incident, he decided to return. In a few days, he arranged his flight and went back to Africa. Chidi was told that electrical faults in the house had caused the fire.

How the fire had started was unknown to Laura and Ogechi, who were at home, plaiting their hair, when the fire broke out. Before the fire was put out, it destroyed most of Chidi's belongings in his room.

Ogechi had gone to Laura's room to get a razor blade when she noticed the smoke was coming out of her brother's room. His room door was always locked since he left for America. Ogechi opened the door to her brother's room only when she wanted to clean the room. So when she saw the smoke, she ran back and told Laura what was happening. Laura was confused and couldn't do anything to save some of her husband's belongings. She could only scream and shout for help. Before the fire service could put out the fire, almost everything in the room was destroyed.

When he was told about the fire, Chidi didn't

know how serious it was until he went home and saw the destruction. The first welcome message he received was that a fire has destroyed most of his belongings. The long-distance journey back home, which should have been a happy moment, turned into a sad moment for him. He had to start life afresh. It took him quite some time to replace the personal belongings he'd lost.

Laura wept bitterly on the day the fire destroyed her husband's room. She began to cry again when she saw her husband was angry about the loss. Chidi was so mad that he accused his wife of being responsible for the fire that had burned his room; unlike him, he scolded her.

"You are just good for nothing. You are a witch. You are the cause of my downfall. Since I married you, you have been inflicting evils on my progress. Let me warn you. I've had enough of you. Any more of this, and I will ask you to leave the house and go back to your father's. I know you are the cause of all these misfortunes. I was doing well before you came here. Once I married you, things were no longer the same. Things began to fall apart for me."

This was the first time Chidi had ever been provoked to anger. When he got to his room and saw that most of his belongings were destroyed, he couldn't believe it. He was absolutely confused and didn't know what to do.

When he realized the nature of the damage in his

room, he became angrier. Ogechi came pleading for him and took his traveling bag from him. She was about to take the bag to Laura's room, but Chidi yelled at her to return the bad to him. He didn't want any of his belongings to enter Laura's room to avoid being afflicted with ill luck. Chidi had a strong belief that Laura had caused every negative thing that had happened to him since he married her. Ogechi quickly returned the bag to him.

It was a terrible day. Chidi thought about leaving the house that night to avoid seeing Laura's face, but he changed his mind for the sake of his children. He stayed home to be with them, whom he had missed for quite some time. While he was still angry, his children came and surrounded him with excitement; they had no clue what their father was going through. The next day, Chidi cooled off, but he didn't forget. He still believed his wife was the cause of his problems.

Chapter 22

TROUBLED TIMES

During their marriage, Chidi and Laura usually visited his in-law with his family since they lived in the same city. One day he came with his family to visit his in-laws as usual. Before they reached their house, they visited different places Laura had never seen before since she was married. She was excited about visiting such importance places for the first time in her life. She had a good time with her husband, but she had no way of knowing that was the last time she would have such fun with him.

After they had finished their visit to other places, they arrived at her parents' home. When they arrived, everybody was at home. The family was happy to see them, and they were well entertained. On the way to his in-laws, Chidi had told Laura he would leave her at her parents' house and then go and see some friends; he would return to pick them up. Laura had wanted to go with him, but he refused and told her they couldn't bring the children with them. So Chidi left her with the children at her parents' house and drove back home under the pretense of going to see his friends.

When he arrived at home, he called his in-laws on the phone and told Mr. Taiwo he was ending his marriage with Laura. She didn't understand what was happening when Chidi called her father and told him their marriage was over. They thought it was a joke until they saw movers arrive at Mr. Taiwo's house with Laura's belongings together with their children's.

Mr. Taiwo couldn't believe it. It was like a daydream. He regarded Chidi's action as a big slap on the face, a mark of contempt. *Perhaps Chidi has gone crazy*, he thought. *This behavior is unlike him.* Chidi had thought about telling his father-in-law about the problem he had been having with his wife. He knew that if he told Mr. Taiwo, his father-in-law would discourage him from taking the action he had taken and that Laura would still be living with him. He didn't want that to happen. He believed Laura was the cause of his problem; once the marriage was over, his downfall would end, and he would start to live a happy life again. Therefore, he felt he had made the right decision to end the marriage.

It was after Chidi had moved Laura's belongings to her father's house that she told her father everything that had happened during her marriage with Chidi.

"The day our house was on fire, he told me that he would put me out of the house if anything like this happened again. I didn't think he was serious until I saw it happen," she explained.

Mr. Taiwo knew Chidi was a responsible man, somebody who always took good care of his family; he'd never heard any complain from him since their marriage. He believed that something greater than what his daughter had told him must have taken place, but he had to hear from Chidi. What his daughter had told him couldn't be the reason for his action. If that was the only reason to end the marriage, something must be wrong with the man. Mr. Taiwo wondered how his daughter could be blamed for the fire that had broken out in the husband's room. He believed the truth would surface sooner or later. He decided to refrain from approaching Chidi for now; he wanted to give him some time to think about his actions. Mr. Taiwo believed issues between husband and wife are often resolved by the couple, not by somebody else. He believed Chidi would later change his mind and come back for his wife and children.

The incident took place when their young son was about to start preschool, but when Chidi didn't come back for his family, Mr. Taiwo started to get more concerned. Laura and her two children had become a burden to her parents. The father had to accommodate them and make provisions for other things the children needed. Laura couldn't go back to work due to her change of location. After two months without hearing from Chidi, Mr. Taiwo tried to work out things with Chidi, to persuade him to take his wife and children back with him, but it didn't work. Then Mr. Taiwo took the matter to court.

Chidi was at home, watching television, when somebody rang his doorbell. He wondered who could be at the door since he hadn't invited anyone to his home. *Perhaps a vendor has brought some newspapers,* he thought.

Ogechi went to see who was at the door. A mailman had come to deliver special mail sent to Chidi. She took the mail to him, told him a man had delivered the mail at the door, and left. Chidi thought it was ordinary mail that didn't require much attention, but it wasn't. When he read the letter, he found out his father-in-law had sued him to court for abandoning his children and the wife with him. Chidi didn't know how serious the matter was, and he failed to act on it. Later, he soon forgot all about it and went on with his life.

On the day he should have reported to court, he didn't show up. A week after the court date, two policemen came to his house to arrest him. When the first came to his place, Chidi wasn't at home. His sister told them Chidi had traveled and would be back in a week.

When Chidi returned, Ogechi told him about the two policemen who had come to look for him. It was then that he remembered the court warrant issued to him a few weeks before. He decided to report to the police station to find out what the warrant was about. When he arrived at the station, the police detained him for failing to report to court on the hearing day.

Ogechi waited for her brother all night, but he didn't come home. She went to the police station to find out what was delaying his return. It was then that she found out the police had detained Chidi. She asked the policeman on duty to see her brother. When she saw him, he told her what had happened and told her to go back home and arrange for a lawyer. After she left the station, she went home and got a lawyer. The next day the lawyer went to the police station and bailed Chidi out.

Later, the case between him and his father-in-law was scheduled in court. After the case was decided, Chidi was found guilty of abandonment and was ordered to pay back the money Mr. Taiwo had spent in taking care of his children and the wife. He was ordered to pay Laura twenty pounds monthly to support the children if he decided to divorce her.

Chidi wasn't satisfied with the judgment. He appealed to another court. The case lingered so long since the court adjourned from time to time. After all the time and money Chidi had spent in pursuing the case, he came to realize that the court system was very frustrating.

Since the case adjourned periodically, Mr. Taiwo also was exhausted. Laura advised her father not to pursue the case anymore, but he refused.

Mr. Taiwo, who was also frustrated with the case, became angry and aggressive over the matter. While the case was still pending, he began to find other means to get with Chidi. Mr. Taiwo had tried other means to hurt him and couldn't succeed; he secretly hired some men to have him kidnapped.

It was the worse period of Chidi's life. He was in a dilemma. He had decided not to have Laura back as his wife again. But her father wanted to force him to take her back. Chidi didn't want to go through the problems with Laura again. He wanted to be left alone.

Chidi began to fear for his life since his father-in-law was threatening to hurt him, so he began to consider leaving town and going to another city where Mr. Taiwo couldn't locate him. To avoid Mr. Taiwo, he did so.

Mr. Taiwo was unable to locate him at the new place where Chidi had moved. During this time, Mr. Taiwo hired some unscrupulous men to make Chidi's life miserable. In one attempt, they smashed his car beyond repair. He ended up having to sell it. After that incident, some of his property was stolen, but the thieves were never caught. The people who were after him had threatened to kill him.

When Chidi realized his life was at stake, he left the township. He spent most of this time in the village to avoid those who were after him. He couldn't live in a permanent place for more than a year. He was definitely afraid for his life. He didn't know who might come after him next; he couldn't identify who his enemies were.

The trouble he faced made him regret coming back to Africa. Chidi started to consider going back to America and living with his friend Mr. Williams in the meantime. After he gave the matter a second thought, he wrote a letter to his friend and explained to him the threat he had received from his father-in-law after he had a misunderstanding with his wife.

Mr. Williams decided to invite him back to America. He invited Chidi to apply for another business visa, and it was granted. When Chidi received the visa, he was relieved. It didn't take long; Chidi began to prepare for his journey to America. During the period he was going through the trial, he didn't disclose his problems to Alice and Chief Ugo, but he kept them to himself.

As he prepared to travel to America, he sent some of his belongings back to the village. His sister carried some of those belongings to the village. When he was ready for the journey, he went to the village with

Ogechi and told his family about his trip to America. He told them he was going to establish a new business with his partner and would soon return. He promised them he would keep in contact with them when he got to America.

Chidi departed and left his two children behind with his mother and father-in-law. It wasn't his plan to leave his children behind, but he believed he had no other choice than to leave the unfriendly environment for now until the situation settled down. Chidi hoped to make peace someday with his wife, mainly because of his children, but when he realized his life was at stake, he decided to escape the land until the trouble subsided. He knew quite well that one day, when his children grew up, they would look for him, and he would reconcile with them. Chidi finally left the village and town behind for a peaceful place.

After Chidi went to America, Ogechi told Alice everything that had taken place while she was living with her brother in the city. It was then that Alice came to understand that Chidi had gone to America to escape the threat from his father-in-law, not because of business, as she had been told. She started to lament.

"Are you saying Chidi went to America to run away from his father-in-law?" Alice asked.

"Yes," Ogechi confirmed.

"Now he has gone. What can we do to bring him back? Nothing! I said nothing. There is nothing we can do to make him come back. Let's pray that he keeps his promise to us. Maybe one day he will return to us," Alice cried.

It didn't take long before Chief Ugo heard about the situation. He lamented as well with great disappointment.

Chapter 23

MEMORIES OF HOME

The hardship Chidi had endured in Africa, compared to the life he was living in America, made him believe Satan had a stronghold in his hometown. Chidi didn't dispute the fact that Satan is everywhere in the world, which includes America, where he had gone to live. But the evil he had seen at home had superseded the evils he'd seen in the land he was visiting. Mr. Williams was a friend, not family; however, he was nice, kind, compassionate, trustworthy, loving, and accommodating. Chidi had never met any person, including family members or relatives in the city or in his village, who had treated him like Mr. Williams did. Instead, dishonesty, hatred, killings, and stealing from one another had become the order of the day. Anything was possible at home.

Sometimes Chidi began to wonder where the human conscience God had given to mankind to do well on earth. More evil people have overshadowed the good ones. The good ones would later join the evil ones, and the outcome became catastrophic. It was the part of the world where the dubious super rich felt good in the misery of the less privileged. Instead of coming together to build their own land, they would rather steal and send their dubious wealth abroad, where it would do no good to anybody at home. Sometimes their wealth would rot in abroad after they had passed away. Nobody in abroad would give account of the stolen money from Africa. Instead, the Europeans would use the money to develop their own land. But no single European had ever stole money from their land and brought it to Africa to hide.

When he went to live in America, Chidi began to experience a new life he had never seen before. He had left the trouble behind him. He could go to sleep without looking over his shoulder for somebody who might come after him. "No wonder this place is called the land of freedom," Chidi said to himself. He could go anywhere he wanted without somebody harassing him.

Before he went there, Chidi hadn't been able to step out of his house in Africa without fear of being attacked by somebody he couldn't even identify. At this time Mr. Williams and his wife gave him a place to stay in their home. He faced some challenges since he arrived. One of those challenges was the cold weather, and the second was the American food he was learning how to eat. It was unlike the local food he was used to back home.

Even though he had been to this place before, it didn't make him friendly with the cold weather and the kind of food he ate there. The cold felt so bad to him that he barely left the house for anywhere. Mr. Williams sometimes took him out to eat. Chidi couldn't identify the type of food he ate compared to the food he'd grown up with in Africa. For the first three months he lived in the United States, the cold weather and the food were big struggles he couldn't cope with.

There was a time when Chidi went out with Mr. Williams to the inner city for sight-seeing; that was when the cold weather had started to recede. They drove through some streets leading to the inner city. Chidi noticed that some of the houses they passed didn't look like the houses in Mr. Williams's neighborhood. These houses were very old and dilapidated. They didn't look like people were living in them.

As they drove closer to the houses, Chidi saw the occupants seating in front of them. They were mainly black people. Since he arrived, Chidi hadn't seen many black people like him in Mr. Williams's neighborhood. It was the first time he'd ever seen his own people in such a large number. The neighborhood didn't look quite like the American neighborhoods Chidi usually saw in those American movies he saw in Africa. The houses in those movies were more glamorous than the one he saw in this neighborhood. The American movies he saw in Africa portrayed the image that nobody was poor in America. But Chidi was surprised to see that not everybody in America was rich, unlike the way the American images were presented in the movies in Africa.

As they drove a little farther down the street, he saw a couple of homeless people begging for money. When Chidi asked Mr. Williams who the people on the street were, he told him they were people who had no place to live. Chidi began to wonder why people like these should be in America, where everybody, especially the Africans, believed every person in America was rich. Chidi didn't see any difference between his own black people who live in America and those living in Africa. Some who lived in Africa even lived in a better house than those he saw in America. The only difference was their environment.

While Chidi was in the city, he met a black man who introduced himself as Melvin Ogunde. Mr. Ogunde's parents had come from Africa, but he was born in America. It was Melvin who helped him locate an African market, where Chidi could purchase some African foods he'd grown up with. It was then that he started to make his own food as it was done back home. He wasn't a great cook, but he was able to cook what he could eat. Back at home, his wife and sister had prepared most of his foods. After buying those food items from the African market, he came to realize that those food items were very expensive; he decided to substitute some of the food with American food to save some money.

The new life in America without his family started to take a toll on him. When he first came to live with Jack Williams he was introduced to the company where Mr. Williams paid him to work. That was how he provided for himself. After he lived in Jack's place for one year, Jack helped him find a place of his own where he had more space.

Chidi had lived in America a little more than one year without a wife, children, or relatives. It hadn't been easy for him, but he had to learn to do everything for himself, which he had never done before while in Africa, especially cooking and washing his own clothes, which his wife had done. Initially when he spoke to Jack Williams about the threat he'd received from his father-in-law, he hadn't told him the whole story. He'd told Mr. Williams that he and his wife were having misunderstandings, which had led her father to threaten him. It was recently that he told Jack about what had happened between him and his wife that caused them to separate. After Mr. Williams learned about Chidi's separation from his wife, he decided to make peace with them.

Chidi was living comfortably and peacefully in

America after he left the problem with his father-in-law behind. At the moment, he wasn't bothered with problems at home. His life in America was much better than the one he'd lived in Africa. Almost everybody he met in America seemed to be nice and kind to him, unlike what went on back in his hometown. People treated one another with disrespect. It seemed that there were more angry people living in the city than in the village. When Chidi had left the city and gone back to his village, it had been more peaceful.

Chidi remembered the day when he went to the market to purchase some new clothes. Two men were quarreling with each other, and the exchange of words turned to cursing at each other. At the beginning, it had seemed like it was a joke, but suddenly, fighting broke out. One broke the other man's nose; blood gushed out of his face. It was then that people came to intervene, and the fight was stopped. The wounded guy was taken out of the scene to be treated.

While the fight initially went on, nobody came to the man's rescue; people watched them fight until one of the fighter's noses was cut open. That was when some people came to stop the fight. This type of violence was very common in the marketplace. Many people had no respect for each another. Chidi had just walked into the market when the fight ended. But he saw a group of people talking about what had happened.

There was a great uproar in the city. The crisis was

greater than a two-man fight. In a state of anarchy, people pry on each other to cause mayhem. That's when the true nature of man's evil comes to play; Chidi remembered the crisis in the city. It was one of its kinds; the devil had come to town. People who seemed to be human beings had turned to monsters; the savagery was great. Blood shed was abundant; properties were looted and destroyed. At the end of the crisis, uncountable lives were lost. In the absence of civil society, the world wouldn't have a place to survive. That was what had happened in the city where Chidi had lived with his boss until peace was restored.

Since he went to America, Chidi hadn't seen anything like what he had seen in Africa, a place where most people took the law into their own hands. He hadn't seen anyone fighting publicly, like in Africa, where fighting happens often. Mr. Taiwo didn't give Chidi the chance to make peace with him because of the threat Chidi was getting from him. He had hired some people to hurt him. The cruelty was so great that he gave up the attempt to reconcile with him. He ran away for his life. Whereas Chidi was trouble free in America, his mind was still at home, where he had left his children. He realized Mr. Williams was a really good friend who always looked after Chidi's good. Since he'd arrived, his friend had been taking good care of him to make him forget his problems at home. Mr. Williams had seen great potential in Chidi.

we do. It is one of the provisions of our constitution for anybody to own a gun," Mr. William said. "People are dying from guns every day. That's the outcome of owing a gun. I believe what is happening in our country with guns today isn't what our forefathers intended when they made the gun law. The gun law was made due to the unsafe environment our forefathers lived in. It was a Wild Wild West then. But today life has changed. We have a stable government that protects its citizens from harm, unlike before when there were crisis and lawlessness going on in our country. Money and politics have made the gun laws come to stay. If not those two things, the gun law would have been eradicated or amended. The presence of guns in our society has made our country more dangerous than ever before. There is no end in sight.

"Many gun owners have been fooled by the gun makers that people must have guns for their own self-protection. But those messages are untrue. If guns weren't available to people, who would kill each other? Probably few would die from minor weapons but not rifles or shotguns. People had to create a market for their products. That's what the gun makers are doing. It's clear that most of these handguns at homes are mainly used by family members to kill one another than the self-protection the gun makers have claimed; yet people haven't learned from the victims of handguns at home."

Mr. Williams had no gun at home; he believed that if God didn't protect people, those who toiled every day to protect themselves were wasting their time. Besides, the gun owners didn't outlive those who didn't have guns; God was the protector of both people. When Mr. Williams had been in Africa on a business mission, he hadn't had the chance to be involved with or committed to any religion other than the work he was sent to do. After he went back to America where he had less to do, he devoted more of his time to the things of the Lord. Both he and his wife were known to be true Christians. They helped people solve their problems. Mr. Williams and his wife had no children of their own, but they helped many families raise their children. They were always ready to bring the gospel to the people around them.

Mr. Williams learned that it was Chidi's superstitious beliefs that had made him to separate from his wife. He had the word of God with Chidi, and that made him to change his mind.

"It is an abomination unto the Lord for a man to leave his wife he had married for another woman with no good justification. All marriages are ordained and made by God. He who made them, made them as one. What God had put together, let no man separate," Jack explained. "It is absolute superstition for someone to reckon with such a belief that someone can bring good or bad luck to somebody. No person can bring bad luck to somebody, but I believe in destiny.

"Whatever God has destined for someone must surely come to pass. If a disaster strikes, that's the handiwork of Satan. 'Commit your way unto the Lord, and you shall be vindicated,'" he said. Chidi was advised that if he committed his ways and problems to God, he would be set free.

After Mr. Williams spoke with him, Chidi began to consider what he had been advised. Chidi later changed his mind and did what he'd been told to do. After that meeting with Mr. Williams, Chidi's life was changed, and he began to commit his life to the things of God. Based on experience with Mr. Taiwo, Chidi thought it would be hard to make peace with him. But Mr. Williams encouraged him to have a change of heart, to make peace with him, and to take his wife and children back. Mr. Williams wasn't concerned about who was at fault between the two. He made it clear to Chidi that the new life he had entered encourages someone to forgive people who have offended him or her.

"If somebody should slap your cheek, turn the other side for another slap," he cited from the Bible. Mr. Williams tried to tell his friend to forgive people

who had done wrong to him, even if he wasn't at fault. "Vengeance is of the Lord," Mr. Williams advised.

Now that Chidi had agreed to make peace with his father-in-law and to retrieve his family to America, Mr. Williams started working to change his status in America. Chidi's professionalism and skill were great resources to Mr. Williams's company so he wanted to retain him in the business. Based on that, Mr. Williams submitted his employment papers to the government authorities to change his business visa into permanent residence so Chidi could work in the company permanently. While the application was in progress, Chidi began to contact his wife and children back in Africa.

It had been more than one year since he last spoke with his wife or children. It was at this time he broke the silence. Chidi called Mr. Taiwo's house; fortunately for him, it was Laura who answered the call. Chidi didn't waste no time; he began to apologize to her for what had happened. He told her he was afraid of coming back to take them with him because of the way her father had threatened to hurt him. Chidi asked Laura to forgive him and promised to come back home to see them and to make arrangements to bring them with him to America.

Laura had mixed feelings when she heard Chidi's voice. The children had missed their father so much. While Laura was talking to him, she became emotional and shed tears. Chidi calmed her down and promised her that everything was going to be all right. At last, she accepted his plea and let go of the past. Chidi asked to speak to his children.

Prince had just turned five. His sister was almost four years old. The young Prince and his sister, Princess Uloma, who had missed their father for a long time, had the chance to speak with him again. After he had finished speaking with them, he promised to be communicating with them frequently.

The next time they spoke again, he had the chance to speak with his father-in-law, Mr. Taiwo. After Chidi hadn't been seen for all those years, his father-in-law had been somewhat concerned about his whereabouts. After Chidi had left his family and went to America, it had become Mr. Taiwo's new responsibility to take care of his grandchildren in the absence of their father. It had become a great burden for him to care for the children. He didn't want to raise the children without their father.

When his daughter told him Chidi had called from American and had wanted to speak with him, her father was willing to speak with him. He had been troubled during the years his daughter and her children had been living with him; it had become a challenge for him to continue to provide for them when they were living with him. He wanted to reach out to Chidi to make peace and so Chidi could take back his wife and children with him, but he couldn't find him anymore.

When he finally spoke with him, he didn't hesitate to accept his apology; they reconciled with each other. Both started a new life afresh. It was then that Chidi told him he would be visiting home to see his wife and children, whom he had missed, and he would let him know when the time came.

Six months had passed since Mr. Williams filed the paper work to change Chidi's status. The government had reviewed his documents. His professional skill had made him to qualify to work and live permanently in America. Based on that, his application for permanent residence was approved by the government. Chidi had just received the approval letter in the mail and was told to expect the main card in the mail in thirty days. After the thirty days came and went, the card arrived. Chidi was granted the authority to live in America permanently with his family.

Now that Chidi had found what he was seeking, he started making plans to travel home and to take his family to America to live with him. He spoke with his wife and her father that he would be coming home in two months. Chidi later departed and went to Africa to meet with his family.

Chapter 24

THE LAST JOURNEY

On the day Chidi arrived, Mr. Taiwo and Laura went to the airport to receive him. Chidi was taken to his father-in-law's house, where he met his children. It was a happy moment for the family. The children and their mother were glad to see their father back home at last.

Chidi had spent four years in America without his family. He had missed his children very much. A few days after he arrived, he met with Mr. Taiwo and his family, including his wife, to apologize to them for what he'd done to his wife. When Mr. Taiwo saw the humility in Chidi's language, he accepted his plea and let go of the past. It was during this meeting that Chidi told them that he would relocate to America with his family.

While Chidi was at Mr. Taiwo's house, he notified his people in the village about his return. His mother and sister were so glad to hear about his arrival back to

Africa after such a long period of time. Chief Ugo had recently died. Nobody had told Chidi about his death, but when they heard he was coming back home, they thought Chidi had come home for his burial.

Chidi was shocked and saddened when he heard about the death of Chief Ugo. He met Amona, who had returned home because of his father's death. It was more than ten years they had not seen each other after their graduation from high school; Chidi had gone to live in the city while Amona joined his cousin in the city to learn how to do business. He lived with the man for five years and was later settled to start his own business. The business didn't do well. He lost some of the seed money he'd started business with. He hadn't visited home for quite some time after he lost most of his money in business. He felt disappointed and shameful whenever he saw his colleagues who had done well in business.

Amona had gone through some difficult times. He didn't have enough to take care of himself and his family including his parents and that of his brothers and sister whom they depend on him to assist them when they need arises. There was no money to bury his father. According to the custom of Umueze, he was obligated to give his father a befitting burial or face the shame. He had borrowed some money from friends, but still it wasn't enough for the burial. Luckily for him, Chidi came at the moment when his help was needed most. It was Chidi who later brought the remaining money for the burial.

Amona was pleased to see his old friend, Chidi, after so many years of not seeing each other. He was very appreciative for many things his friend had done for his father, including the house he'd built for his father while he was alive. Amona knew that what Chidi had done for his father was his responsibility, but since Amona couldn't afford to do what Chidi had done, he couldn't be blamed. In fact, Amona had done what a man should do to make life better for his family, but his efforts had proved futile.

The desire was out of kindness and appreciation that Chidi could render the help to Chief Ugo. He did remember that it was Chief Ugo who had helped him finish his secondary school after his father died. His contributions to the burial were the right thing to do. The burial responsibilities, which the village custom had imposed on the first sons of Umueze, were a bad custom. Even those who couldn't afford to bury their fathers were forced by the village custom to borrow money to fulfill the tradition. Chidi remembered being in the same situation after his father died. The village had demanded a befitting burial for his father.

"A befitting burial was given to my father," Chidi recalled. "The burial took place when I was too young to understand what was happening. It was unnecessary to waste so much to bury the dead."

The money that was wasted in the burial could have been used to complete Chidi's education, but after that money was spent, he was unable to finish his school. What had happened to Chidi had been a double loss. He'd lost his father and, at the same time, the chance to attend the university. The college dream his father had had for him when he was alive didn't come true. Chidi ended up not attending the college he'd been promised.

"A lot was lavished on my father's burial ceremony. After the event, my family suffered greatly. My ambition to further my education was paralyzed. My father had enough to train me, but his burial swallowed all his wealth, which led to the end of my school. I was subjected to all sorts of hardship and suffering." Chidi recollected.

I dislike people who take so much interest in lavishing money on burials. Any custom that encourages expensive burial ceremony should be abolished. Allow the dead to bury themselves," Chidi said with a frown.

The burial event of Chief Ugo came and went. It was celebrated like that of his friend, Chief Udo. After the burial was over, Chidi met with Alice and Ogechi and told them he would be returning permanently to America with his family. He advised them to take good care of the house in the village and assured them that he would be visiting home occasionally.

During their meeting, he told his sister to prepare for the entrance examination to the university. He left enough money for her school and other things needed for the house. He promised to pay for her university education. Chidi wanted to put his sister through college, which nobody had obtained in his family before. He also thought about putting himself through college as well after settling with his family in America; he had never had the chance to attend college when he was young. He would be able to do that when he got back to America.

Before Chidi and his family returned to the city and his father-in-law's house, they had to spend some time in the village after Chief Ugo was buried. Back in the city, Chidi began to prepare for their journey. After the family's traveling documents were completed, he had to contact Jack Williams and let him know the day they were supposed to leave home for America. Mr. William had to wait for them to arrive on that day.

Two weeks later, Chidi and his family departed to America. Mr. Taiwo and his wife, Margaret, drove them to the airport. They arrived at the airport a little early to have enough time to check in their luggage. They were the first people to arrive and to check in their bags. Before the checking began, Mr. Taiwo and his wife had the chance to spend the last moment with their grandchildren and their mother.

As the family left them to enter the plane, Margaret

UCHE N. KALU

was filled with emotion and began to cry; the daughter couldn't resist and also cried. Chidi came back and held Laura, pleading with her not to cry. It was at that moment that he promised Margaret that he and her daughter would keep in touch with them after they arrived in America. At the point of entry, they walked straight into the plane. It took them the same distance Chidi had gone when he came back home after being in America.

Before they arrived, Mr. Williams and his wife, Elizabeth, were already waiting for them at the airport to pick them up. It was a long trip. Everybody was exhausted, especially the children. At the airport, Chidi introduced his wife and the children to Mr. Williams and his wife. They later drove together to Chidi's new apartment. They were glad to see Chidi and his family. His friends joyfully welcomed them to America.